BEFORE YOU GO

BEFORE

YOU GO

A NOVEL BY JAMES PRELLER

FEIWEL AND FRIENDS | NEW YORK

For Lisa and Nick

A FEIWEL AND FRIENDS BOOK
An Imprint of Macmillan

Library of Congress Cataloging-in-Publication Data Available

ISBN: 978-0-312-56107-9

Book design by PHIL FALCO

Feiwel and Friends logo designed by Filomena Tuosto

First Edition: 2012

10 9 8 7 6 5 4 3 2 1

macteenbooks.com

"The stars are not wanted now, put out every one."
—W. H. AUDEN, "FUNERAL BLUES"

THE ACCIDENT

This is the moment between *before* and *after,* the pivot point upon which story, like a plate, spins.

See:

Two cars drive down a bleary road. One headed east, the other west. A small animal moves from the shadows to paw the asphalt. Not thirty seconds sooner, nor a moment later, but exactly now.

To the eastbound driver, traveling alone after a long night, the animal appears only as a dreamlike shape, two red eyes floating in the misty wash of headlights. He veers to avoid it and in doing so drifts into the approaching lane.

Music plays from the westbound car, intermixed with teenage voices, laughter. Eyes widen when the car swerves toward them. The driver jerks the wheel and the car cuts counterclockwise, careens across the left lane. A foot stomps the brake pedal, back tires lock and skid, loose gravel sprays from the wheels. The side of the car crashes against a mighty oak

1

that has stood undisturbed for over one hundred years. The front passenger's door collapses inward, its metal panel crushed like a paper cup.

It happens fast. The span of a heartbeat, the time it takes to squeeze a hand, to shut your eyes and . . . nothing. Blood flows, bones shatter. It is the slice of a razor: when before becomes after, when everything changes.

And all the king's horses, and all the king's men . . .

There is a moment of stunned disbelief, an absence of movement, the vacuum suck of unreality. The music still plays like the soundtrack to a frozen photograph: a car on the side of the road wrapped around a tree, broken windows, mangled metal, the cold-eyed moon indifferent; a recorded voice bounces off a satellite to sing about a town that seems so hopeless.

After a pause, the summer bugs start in again, the buzz of cicadas, a cricket, the croak of a bullfrog from a muddy pond. Now the screaming begins from inside the car, drowning out the other night noises. Hysterical, high-pitched, piercing. The driver's side rear door flies open, a figure staggers out from the backseat. The figure turns, eyes wild and unseeing, falls to both knees in the middle of an empty road on a warm, wet, shimmering summer night, battered head in bloodied hands.

Movement appears from inside nearby homes. Shadows cross behind the panes, curtains shudder. A door opens and a shaft of light spills to the ground, stumbling like a drunk on the sidewalk. Phones are found, numbers punched, 9-1-1.

Hurry. An emergency. Car accident. Hit a tree. Hard to see, sounds bad. Morgan Road, please hurry. Woke up to a crash and screaming, terrible screaming.

Come and stop the screaming.

Two of the four passengers will walk away with minor injuries. *A miracle,* some will say. *Thank God, thank God almighty.* The third will suffer a concussion, three broken ribs, cuts, and bruises. The injuries will not be fatal.

The final passenger, who sat in the shotgun seat opposite the driver, never had a chance. Death came instantly, like a curtain closing, a theater turning black.

The night animal scurries into the underbrush, its role in the passion play complete. One car races unscathed into the distance, hurtling east like a bullet from a gun. Taillights dim, then fade. The crashed vehicle plays a song from the radio.

This town, it seems so hopeless, so hopeless.

That's the scene when you run out of miracles. The light, the light just disappears.

PART ONE: BEFORE

ONE

Jude squeezed his eyes shut, blinking away the sun's glare, and waited for the eight-fifteen-in-the-freaking-morning bus. On a Saturday, no less. The stop was located beneath the elevated Long Island Rail Road, with rails that hummed overhead and stretched across the length of the island, connecting the farthest points east all the way to Pennsylvania Station in Manhattan. For as long as he could remember, New York City had beckoned to Jude, offering an exotic world of freedom and possibility. The city stood as a skyscrapery refutation of his suburban life, escape only a train ticket and forty-five minutes away.

He sat cross-legged on the curb, leaned back on his hands, and scanned the road for coming traffic. Most people around here drove like psychopaths, and Jude wasn't eager to have his legs run over. It might ruin his weekend, the bleeding stumps, all that dragging around. Better, he thought, not to get run over in the first place, so he cast a wary eye down the road. Today was the first day of the rest of his life, and Jude would spend it at Jones Beach—starting a new summer job in the food-service industry. There were still a couple of weeks of school left and the grind of finals, but they needed workers on weekends, and Jude wasn't in a position to make anybody wait. Jobs weren't easy to find, and his skills, Jude had discovered, were not highly in demand, as he had none.

Barely awake, he had dressed in the required uniform of black pants and orange T-shirt. Because naturally you wear black pants to the sun-baked beach. Jude Fox was on his way to becoming a minimum-wage flunky, a burger-grilling, soda-spilling concession-stand worker.

The morning sun shone not high above the horizon, garish and bright, so Jude stepped back into the station's cool cement shadows. It was going to be a hot one, the first scorcher of summer—not a cloud in sight, just blue June skies. In truth, Jude didn't hate the idea of working. He'd heard that beach jobs could be okay, even fun. But Jude was a realist; he knew it would basically blow. Or suck. Strange how those two words, *blow* and *suck*, both conveyed the same and yet totally different meanings. It blew, it sucked: same thing. Weird. He'd heard people complain about their jobs all his life. Why should his job be any different? So he couldn't help but wonder if getting a job had been a colossal mistake. Sometimes it felt to Jude that he was just like those trains overhead, traveling between two steel rails, the course of his life mapped out long ago. No steering wheel, no brakes. Jude followed the path carved out for him, no different from anybody else.

These are the thoughts you have when you wake up too early on a Saturday morning.

Jude had taken this particular bus many times before, usually with a murder of boys dressed in shorts or baggy bathing suits, with beach towels rolled in tubular fashion or backpacks slung over their shoulders. They went to hang in the sand, admire the girls, swim if the jellyfish weren't too bad, wander the boardwalk, and later, catch a bus home, sunburned and happy.

A few glassy-eyed stragglers gathered at the stop, mostly young beach workers in Halloween colors. It was too early for the leather-skinned beach crowd. Jude knew a few of the guys at the stop, not interested in talking, so did the chin-lift thing. They were all in the same boat as Jude—or, very soon, the same bus; the learner's permit crowd, old enough to work an entry-level job, not old enough to drive there.

Jude had considered running to the beach, about seven miles door to door, but that would've required setting his alarm even earlier, and then he'd need a place to shower once he got there. His body could absorb a run like that no problem, but it could make for a long day if work turned out to be tough. Maybe another time, after he scoped out the job situation. His dad was already up and out, gone for the day. Jude had half hoped his mother would offer to give him a lift, step up this one time, but he knew not to count on miracles. As a matter of personal policy, Jude kept his expectations low to avoid disappointment. That was the strategy, anyway.

A good-looking girl whom Jude knew a little bit showed up, the beautiful Dani Remson with long legs that went all the way up to her shoulders. She'd had a brief thing with his friend Corey about six months back. Something about Dani had always made Jude uneasy, maybe because she was a predatory goddess with brown eyes that lasered right into him. So, head down, Jude busied himself with the apps on his cell, and that worked sufficiently well. After a teasing, sing-songy, "Mooorning, Jude," Dani brushed past him to join another girl who stood clutching a can of Diet Pepsi.

The bus came and everybody shuffled onboard, feet dragging. Jude grabbed a seat toward the back, stuffed in earbuds, found the Cure on his iPod, gazed out the window for the ride south on Wantagh Parkway. Jude had been obsessing over the Cure lately, especially the best tunes off *Disintegration*. As a band, they peaked in the early 90s, but Jude liked them anyway. Music was music; it didn't matter if a song was made fifty years ago in Liverpool, England, or behind some guy's woodshed five minutes ago. The good tunes *stuck* and the rest dropped away. Some days Jude could listen to "Pictures of You" on an endless repeat cycle, losing himself in the interplay of guitar, synthesizer, and bass. That the Cure's songs were often dark, brooding, and melancholy only made it all the better. Jude didn't really go for the Cure's poppier, radio-ready numbers. He had played guitar for eight years now, practicing four, five times a week. Guitar was his retreat. It was a door closing, shutting the world out, and a window opening, connecting him to something *other*, a rift in space through which he escaped for hours at a time. Jude felt, not without reason, that music had saved his life. But, hey, music made *everything* better—even bus rides to a particular version of sucks called My First Day on the Job.

The bus dropped the passengers off near the huge traffic circle at Central Mall, Field Four. This was the busiest, most crowded, commercial area of Jones Beach, loosely divided into fields. The famous Jones Beach watertower signaled a visitor's entrance to the beach. The iconic tower thrust skyward at more than 225 feet. It dominated the flat horizon like an extended middle finger. Young children called it the pencil, usually in a happy squeal, for it announced their arrival. *Here you go, happy beachgoers, now pay your parking fee and grab a patch of sand.*

Jude turned his back to the tower and walked toward the boardwalk like everybody else in sight—it was either that or step into traffic—then turned right to wind his way to operation headquarters where he'd been told to check in. The building wasn't much, a trailer on steroids obscured by a scraggle of bushes, tucked behind the men's bathroom. Jude noted that it offered showers and lockers, definitely useful if he ever wanted to run to work some morning.

He hesitated in the open doorway, looking in at a thin, middle-aged man dressed in a white short-sleeved shirt and dark tie seated behind a gray metal desk. The man, obviously a boss-type individual, had sinewy arms covered in thick curly hair, like some kind of tree-climbing forest creature. His jaw muscles worked on a stick of gum. A nameplate on the desk read KEATING. No dummy, Jude took that for the guy's name. Keating spoke into his phone in fits and spurts, listening impatiently before barking out directives such as, for example, "We've got to get those freezers fixed, or we'll have fifteen god-damned hundred pounds of melted chopped beef on our hands!" If he noticed Jude's presence, Keating didn't bother to glance up. Even after snapping shut the phone, Keating continued to ignore Jude, concentrating instead on working his gum while tapping a pencil against the side of his head.

Tap, tap, tap. Anybody home?

Jude recognized Keating's performance for what it was, a random, unnecessary, and totally unimpressive display of power. So Jude said, "Yeah, hi, excuse me, I was—"

Keating raised a hand for silence. "Grab some bench, son. The car'll be back in a few minutes. Where you going?"

"Going?" Jude asked. "I just got here."

Keating raised his chin to give Jude a long look. The career food-service manager was lean and square-jawed, a wiry man, a runner no doubt, and he chomped on gum as if it had hurt his feelings. One of those marathoner guys Jude saw every-where filling the roadways in his neighborhood, galloping down the street as if they were chasing immortality. His own father was one of them.

"This your first day?" Keating asked.

"Yeah, *yes*," Jude said, pulling some rumpled papers from his back pocket. "They told me to—"

"And you are? . . ."

That stumped Jude for a second. He wavered, befuddled. Jude's mind didn't at first recognize it as a question, so he stood like a lowland gorilla, waiting for Keating to finish the sentence, tell Jude what he was, exactly, before finally answering, "Fox, Jude Fox."

"You sure about that, son? You need more time to think about it?" Keating cracked. He reached for Jude's papers as if they'd been soaked in poison. Unsmiling, he poured coffee down his throat and unsmiled some more.

Things were going just swell.

Jude shifted on his feet, glancing around at the grim, cluttered office. It truly was nothing more than a transformed trailer. Jude hated this whole scene already with a passion he usually reserved for chemistry teachers, party clowns, and the Grammys. Worst of all, Jude was pretty sure he wasn't getting paid yet. So all this pleasant chitchat came absolutely free.

Keating's phone chimed the opening riff to some Billy Joel tune—"We Didn't Start the Fire"—and the man paused before answering. He jerked a thumb, gesturing outside. "Like I said. Find some pine, sit on it, and we'll get to you." Keating didn't need to call Jude a dumb-ass; it was implicit.

Jude took a couple of steps back, more than happy to get away from the runty marathoner and his Napoleon complex.

Outside, there wasn't a chair in sight; confused, Jude looked back at Keating.

"Around the corner," Keating said. Then he grumbled into the phone, "It's a parade of lost lambs around here, yeah, yeah,"—he laughed like a toothy hyena at some joke— "everybody's looking for new talent. Right now all's I got is a couple of guys with that deer in the headlights look. I'll send you what I got."

TWO

There was another kid waiting on the far end of the bench. He was fattish, and splotches of sweat already darkened his orange T-shirt. The boy sat with his shoulders against the trailer office, arms folded across his chest, legs stretched out, ankles crossed, wearing red sneakers with bright green laces. His expression said that he wasn't thrilled to be here and didn't care who knew it.

"Hey," Jude said almost inaudibly.

The boy stirred, uncrossed his ankles. "Sucks, doesn't it?" he grumbled. "Sitting here, hot as hell."

Jude squinted at the climbing sun. He shrugged. "I hear when it rains, they tell you not to come in to work. We only make money when the weather's good."

"Got that right," the boy said. He reached out a hand. "My name is Roberto and I'm a workaholic."

"I try to lay off the workahol myself," Jude said. "That stuff'll mess with your mind."

Roberto laughed. "Workahol, that's funny."

Jude smiled, asked, "This your first day?"

"First day, second year," Roberto answered. "I reenlisted. I still can't believe I took this job again—even my grandmother laughs at me. You know what that feels like? When even your mawmaw thinks you're a joke? Damn. Everybody knows I hate the beach. The sun, the crowds, the seagulls. Sand everywhere. You never get it out of your hair, *ever.* Growing up, it was the last place I wanted to be. Now I work here. God's big joke and I'm the punchline."

Jude gestured to the trailer. "I guess you know Mr. Sunshine."

"Keating?" Roberto said. "Don't worry, you won't see much of him. Did he tell you what field you're working?"

"No," Jude said. "He told me to sit on the bench."

Roberto explained that there were different concession buildings up and down the beach: Field Six, Central Mall, the Bathhouse, Field Two, Zack's Bay, a few others. He quickly ran through the pros and cons of each one. "Field Six is dead, so that can be good *and* bad. You don't have to work hard, but it's boring as hell. Mostly moms with dark tans, fake boobs, and little kids. Plus, some old people who never bother to walk down to the water. They set up folding chairs right on the edge of the parking lot and bake in the sun like raisins. They never eat anything, just wander in looking for napkins and free ice," he said. "Central Mall, right here, is a mob scene, busy all the time, and it's right next to headquarters, so the white shirts like Keating are in and out all day for surprise inspections."

"'Surprise inspections,' what's that?"

"It's when the big shots show up unannounced. They love to strut around like peacocks, you know, feathers in their butts, point out ridiculous crap nobody cares about, ketchup containers almost empty, the heat's too high on the grill, too many boxes lying around, what the F ever—it's their big chance to boss around a bunch of teenagers, basically. Chat up some of the pretty girls."

Jude nodded. He enjoyed listening to Roberto almost as much as Roberto liked talking.

"And just pray you don't get stuck at Zack's Bay," Roberto said emphatically. "That place is like another planet, believe me."

"So where *do* I want to work?" Jude asked.

Roberto held up crossed fingers. "West End Two," he said. "It's way out there, almost at Long Beach, not far from where they shot the tollbooth scene in *The Godfather.* Remember that, when Sonny got shot, like, fifteen million times?"

Jude remembered. You spend any time on Long Island, somebody's bound to point out those tollbooths where Sonny got shot.

Roberto continued, "It's a fifteen-minute drive from here, so if one of the bosses decides to pull a surprise inspection, we'll get a call from our spies before he's even in the car. But the best thing about West End Two? I hear that Kenny 'Half-Baked' Mays is back as closing manager—working for that guy's a trip and a half."

A few minutes later, they were on their way. A different supervisor had picked them up—Jude guessed it was his job to taxi around different workers to the far-flung concession stands. This guy was thick and fiftyish. He wore tinted, wire-rimmed glasses, a ten-gallon hat, and told the boys he was new to the area, originally from Houston, Texas. He had that avuncular Southern thing going full blast, so he blabbed the whole ride over. "Call me Ed," he instructed the boys, "Big Ed, Eddie, I don't give a rat's patootie." He looked into the rear-view mirror at Jude. "You met Mr. Keating this morning, huh?"

Jude nodded cautiously.

"So what'd you think?" Big Ed inquired.

Jude knew a trap when he fell into one. "We didn't really get a chance to, um—"

Big Ed laughed, a hearty whoop. "You know what we say about guys like him back where I'm from? He's all hat and no cattle."

Roberto laughed out loud, smiling and bobbing his head at Jude. "I like that, Big Ed. All hat and no cattle."

"Texas is a great place for expressions, lots of colorful people back there," Big Ed mused.

"So how'd you end up here?" Jude asked.

"That's the $64,000 question, ain't it?" Big Ed replied. He looked out the driver's side window, clicked his wedding ring on the steering wheel, and his wondering eyes scanned the dunes and the ocean beyond it, as if looking for something that wasn't there. "I guess it was time to go, simple as that. Besides, I'm near retirement. Time for a new beginning."

It was a nice ride. Big Ed was a good guy, laid-back and quick to laugh. He talked to Jude and Roberto as if they were equals. Big Ed was a boss and they knew it; he didn't need to club 'em over their heads with it. Best of all, Big Ed dropped them off at West End Two. "Work hard, boys," he called after them in a Texas lilt, "from can till can't. You ever need a lift, give Big Ed a shout."

THREE

Roberto led the way through the back door, which opened from the parking lot into a gray room about the size of a train car, cluttered with shelves, metal tables, and boxed goods of every size. No one seemed to be around.

Acting as tour guide, Roberto pointed to various doors and explained that they opened to closet-size storage rooms, a large walk-in refrigerator (with kegs of beer), a freezer, and the manager's office. Though the door was partially open, Roberto knocked on it and waited.

The manager's name was Denzel Jessup—no lie. He recognized Roberto from the previous summer, when Roberto spent a week filling in over at Field Six. Jessup had the look of a thoroughbred: tall, taut, broad-shouldered, dark-skinned. As manager, he earned the right to wear a white button-down shirt and a cheap black tie. Somehow on Jessup it looked almost sharp. He stood tall, acting neither friendly nor unfriendly; kept it neutral, all business. It took Jessup about a minute and a half to casually let drop that he was an upperclassman at an Ivy League school, that he was too smart for this shit, and that if everybody did their jobs, it would all go fine and he wouldn't have to crawl into anybody's ass.

Jude would spend the rest of the summer trying to purge that disgusting image from his mind.

Jessup grabbed a clipboard and filled out time cards for the new employees. He exhaled heavily, obviously bored, and intoned, "I'll say this once, so listen up. This is your time card. It's how you get paid. Unless you are doing this job for free out of your deep love for fast food, mouse crap, and cooking grease, you will need to keep track of your hours." He put a hand on a clunky, square clock mounted to the wall. "This is the time clock. Are you following me so far?"

"Time card, mouse crap. Got it," Jude said.

Jessup titled his head to look at Jude, as if he wasn't sure he liked what he heard. His eyes flickered with cool assessment. "Do not check in before your assigned starting time," Jessup continued. "Not if you arrive five minutes early, not if you arrive two minutes early. If your shift starts at ten, that's when you punch in. Got it?"

Jude nodded. It wasn't hard to get.

The building itself was basically a large square box, divided by a long, chest-high counter that ran across its length. On the far side of the counter, there was an open area for the public to mill around, search through squat freezer cases for ice cream, line up for hot food. There were also a few wire display containers with bags of chips, Doritos, Cracker Jacks, that kind of stuff. Beyond that there was a row of five cashier booths, where customers paid good money for bad food.

The walls at the front of the high-roofed building were made completely of glass, offering an open view of the big sky, the beach, and the Atlantic at least two hundred yards beyond. West End was a huge beach; it was a long, hot trek to the water. A few people sat at round, yellow picnic tables, shaded by green umbrellas. Mostly indolent girls in bikinis, sipping on straws, watching their napkins blow away in the breeze.

Things were slow, Jessup explained, since it was only a little after ten o'clock, but it would pick up soon. A skeleton crew of six worked on the business side of the counter. During peak hours, as many as twelve orange-shirted laborers crammed behind it. There was a long grill for burgers and hot dogs, a pizza oven, one of those glass warming boxes for soft pretzels, a couple of deep fryers for popcorn chicken, French fries, and onion rings. There was a place to serve soda and beer. Jessup paused there. "In New York State, you must be twenty-one to serve alcohol. You must be twenty-one to drink it." He looked directly at Jude. "If I catch you stealing so much as a sip of beer while I'm on duty, you're gone. I will fire your ass, and I will not blink twice. Got it?"

"Yep." Jude nodded. But even so, it was pretty cool to have cold beer right there, free-flowing from those silver taps. Jude liked beer, more or less, but didn't love it, though it wasn't something he admitted out loud. Jude guessed a lot of guys felt the same way—all standing around, phony as Monopoly money, taking their first sips of beer, faking it. And though he'd been around it enough, Jude usually passed on the opportunity to get plastered and throw up on himself. He figured it might be in his blood, that one day he'd get all slurry and puke-faced, but he wasn't in a hurry to get there. Jude didn't like the idea of losing control, bumping into things, falling down face-first. He thought of his mother. She hadn't taken a drink in six years. But he still remembered when she did. Mom and her cocktails. She didn't drink for fun back then— it wasn't about good times for dear old Mom—and it never ended pretty.

"Almost forgot," Jessup said. "Here are your hats. Wear them at all times when you're working the counter."

He handed the boys two flat, folded pieces of thick white paper. Roberto pulled it open and stuck it on his head. The hat didn't sit well on his squarish skull. He eyed himself in the reflection of a glass fridge.

Jude laughed at him. "Dude, that's a bad look."

"You kidding?" Roberto said, face brightening. "On a guy like me, with the shape of my face? This hat is a babe magnet. Those girls out there will see me in this hat and think, *Fat guy, paper hat, I gotta get me some of that.* It's all over, fellas. I'm going to be punching fresh numbers into my cell all day long." He tapped an index finger into his palm for emphasis.

"Save a few girls for the rest of us, huh?" Jessup said, finally loosening up.

Jude held the hat in front of him. "Do we *really* have to wear these?"

"This is food service," Jessup said, no longer smiling. "Heads must be covered. It's state law."

"What if I wore, like, a baseball cap," Jude ventured, "or some other kind of—"

"Oh, you mean, as a way to express your individuality?" Jessup asked. "Would you prefer a red beret? You want to stand out from the rest of the crew?"

"Actually, I was thinking of something a little less hardcore dork," Jude offered.

Jessup laughed. "Put on the paper hat, Mr. Fox, and welcome to West End Two."

FOUR

The next few hours rolled in like a big wave, a tsunami of new responsibilities. The work crew grew in size—a diverse group of characters, white, black, Hispanic, all young, all wearing paper hats—and yet they soon grew overwhelmed by the demands of the hungry, sun-kissed hordes. The customers came in droves, tanned and muscular, gorgeous and lean, fat and T-shirted, wanting burgers, wanting drinks, wanting service, now, now, now.

Jude spent a long stretch hunched over the hamburger grill beside a more experienced worker, Billy Motchsweller, curly-haired and rail thin, with lightning-fast, caffeine-fueled hands. Sweat dripped off Jude's face, ran off the tip of his nose like a leaking faucet. On Billy's instructions, Jude hustled to the back for more burgers, trays of buns. But he didn't know where those things were kept, got turned around, made wrong guesses, wasted time, and pissed off Billy. "No, no, not these, shit for brains. These burgers are frozen solid." He grabbed two patties and clanged them together to make his point. "Go to the back fridge, not the freezer up front. There should be burgers that were thawed out last night. . . ."

Jude nodded and hurried and earnestly tried not to screw up. He'd bump into someone, knock a drink out of another's hand, slip on the greasy floor, and feel confused and pathetic. Of course, Billy was mistaken; no one had thought to thaw out the burgers last night, hauling the boxes from the freezer to the fridge. Billy shrugged. "Then let's fire up those hockey pucks. It's not like we've got a choice."

Jude now had to pry apart the burgers, chopping at them with a knife while trying not to cut off any of his ten digits. He lined the burgers up in rows on the grill, straight columns of five up and down. At the peak times, there were up to forty burgers cooking at once—sizzling, thawing, bleeding, burning. At the side nearest Billy, the burgers were completely cooked; at the other, raw and hard red discs. Meanwhile, Jude had to open and arrange the buns to meet Billy's precise specifications. He preferred the bun warmed, not burned. Billy moved like a Japanese hibachi chef, flashing his silver spatula with dazzling dexterity. The guy was fast, a gunslinger of the Wild West. Billy made it look easy, piling up paper plates with burgers, yelling, "Come on, take it and move along!" verbally prodding customers on their way like cattle.

"Fun, huh?" bloodshot Billy commented right in the middle of the worst of it, the building packed with people. Jude could see that it wasn't a joke. Billy enjoyed the frenzied scramble, the long lines of beef-starved customers. "Time flies when you're in the weeds," Billy told Jude. "You'll get used to it."

When Billy disappeared to take a break, it was Roberto's turn to wilt over the hot grill. Jude worked at his side, on bun detail. Jude figured he wouldn't touch another burger for at least a year, maybe two. Working with fast food does that to a guy. Nothing kills an appetite faster than an overweight kid with a spatula.

Thing is, nobody cared—business boomed. The sun-dried mob demanded grease for their gullets. People were out of their minds with hunger, and the concession stand was the only source of food on the horizon.

Roberto paused to take a drink. "Damn, it's hotter than Hoth around here."

"Hoth?" Jude asked.

"Ironic *Star Wars* reference," Roberto explained. "A planet covered with ice and snow, native creatures include the tauntaun and the wampa. The Rebel Fleet had a base there, code name Echo."

"Oh my God," Jude said as he realized it, "you're a *Star Wars* geek."

"*Was*," Roberto said. "Now I'm more of a Comic-Con kind of guy. But, yeah, definitely. I'm into all that stuff, Dungeons and Dragons, anime—"

Jessup stopped by, tapped Jude on the shoulder. "Ivan will take your spot. I want you to work security."

"You're putting this skinny guy on security?" Roberto chimed in, smiling broadly. "Oh, this'll be good."

"What?" Jude asked. He didn't know what any of it meant.

"We're getting ripped off blind," Jessup observed.

Jude glanced out at the crowd of milling customers. He could see that it was probably true, teenage boys concealing food under their towels, or snarfing down hot dogs before they reached the cashier.

"Seriously?" he asked. "What am I supposed to do?"

"You're the new guy, Mr. Fox. Do you want to keep your job, or do I need to find somebody else?" Jessup was once again enjoying his position of authority.

So Jude followed his manager into the open area, a few feet before the row of cashiers, amid the slow-moving clutter of customers. "Okay, stand here. Spread your feet like this." Jessup kicked at Jude's feet. "Cross your arms and look like you mean business."

Jude felt embarrassed, sensed a few of the cashiers watching from behind. He didn't like to be made to look foolish. It stung.

"It's prevention," Jessup explained. "Don't worry. If they see you, most people won't try anything."

"What do I do if I catch somebody?"

"Just ask 'em to put it back," Jessup said. "Trust me. No-body will mess with a tough guy like you."

Jude stood about four inches shorter and fifty pounds lighter than Jessup. "Look at me," Jude said. "I'm not going to scare anybody. You really think they're going to listen to me?"

Jessup didn't answer, just returned to his office behind the counter.

Roberto called out to Jude, "Hey, Jude! Hey, Judy, Judy! Don't stress, my brother, if there's any trouble, we got your back!" The way he laughed along with Ivan and a couple of other guys, Jude was pretty sure the exact opposite was true.

There wasn't much to it, actually. Jude wasn't a security guard by nature; he wasn't going to go out of his way to catch offenders. But Jessup was right—by merely standing *there,* a frowning presence, Jude deterred most of the amateur felons, the hot-dog wranglers and burger burglars. The cashiers behind him received a steady flow of customers. Jude caught one cashier in the middle booth watching him with a look of amusement. Her eyes were wide set; her hair, black whorls and corkscrews and curlicues. Skin olive-inflected and smooth. Jude grinned, a little goofily, and she gave him a sympathetic shrug.

Each cashier at West End Two was female—it must have been corporate policy. A large, lumpen girl was stationed at the extreme left cashier's booth—Jude hadn't learned her name yet; Billy hadn't bothered to give Jude the lowdown on her, unlike the others—and she sat, frowning and bored, obviously miserable, with all the charisma of a garden slug. Daphne was next, a pale small blonde with bee-stung lips and dark bags under her eyes. She was either sick, undernourished, or a future runway model. Roberto had already joked that he couldn't decide whether he wanted to bang Daphne or rush her to the emergency room. Which was pretty funny if you asked

Jude. The girl in the middle booth, aside from a few glances Jude's way, worked steadily. Billy had told Jude her name. *What was it again?* Jude remembered: Becka something. She looked great without trying, smiled at patrons, competent at her job. The fourth booth was closed, with a girl named Kath at the farthest booth to the right. There was something unnerving about her, with frizzy black hair, large bust, and tight pants. Even from a distance, everything about her cried, *"loves sex."* No, that wasn't entirely true. Because after her body cried *"loves sex,"* the expression on her face added, *"but not with you."* This made her an early target of fascination among the guys behind the counter. Honestly, she scared the bejeezus out of Jude. Kath looked like the black widow of minimum-wage cashiers.

Trouble took the forbidding form of three tattooed body-builders, ridiculously jacked guys with military haircuts. College guys, probably, former high school football players, almost certainly. Jude watched as they piled cardboard trays high with burgers, pizza, soft drinks, and pretzels. Gathered in front of Jude, out in the open for everyone to see, they began to wolf down the food before reaching the cashiers. Their arrogance annoyed Jude; they didn't even try to hide it. Jude stepped toward them, and in the friendly tone of a co-conspirator suggested that maybe they try to be more subtle about it. You know, wink-wink, *keep it on the down low.* He explained that it was his job to work security, and he hoped they'd understand.

The biggest one, with pectorals the size of hubcaps, swiveled his thick neck to Jude and said, "Huh? What?"

Jude glanced from this Cro-Magnon to his steroidal buddies. "I'm just saying, could you maybe try to be more discreet about it. It's my first day on the job and—"

The mouth-breathing behemoth, under heavy lids and dead eyes, finished chomping on his burger. His hands were huge. He swilled a large soda. "I'm still hungry," he growled to his pals, smacking one of them in the chest. "Food here sucks, though. Right?"

"Yeah, you shouldn't eat that stuff." Jude forced a chuckle, interjecting himself into the conversation (such as it was). "People have actually *died* from eating those burgers." Jude really, really didn't want to get punched in the face. But at the same time, some shred of dignity kept him from backing off.

The mouth breather grew tired of Jude's presence. He defiantly stuffed half of a soft pretzel into his gaping gob. "Whaddayagonnadoaboutit?" he challenged Jude. Very *Jersey Shore*. Then he did the puffy-chest dance that guys like him do, his shoulders stiffening, one step forward into Jude's space, a vein in his forehead pulsing with animal hostility. It was a dance he had probably performed hundreds of times—before pummeling his hapless victims. Jude wondered if his adversary took human-growth hormone. Or horse steroids. Or whatever else those weight lifters took to grow so freakishly scary-looking.

How had he gotten himself into this mess?

Jude glanced toward the front counter; Roberto cautiously inched around the corner. He had a spatula still in his hand, as if it might be an effective weapon. He might as well have been carrying a flyswatter.

A voice called out from behind Jude. "Hey, you guys, come on, hurry up, this way."

It was the middle cashier, Becka, gesturing impatiently to the trio of bodybuilders. She waved them through the line, moving them along quickly. She looked across the room for any sign of Jessup, then said to Jude, "It's okay, these guys already paid."

The three incredible hulks, agog and somewhat bewildered, shuffled their way past the line and out of the building. "Yeah, what she said," one of them muttered, looking back scornfully at Jude.

"Are you out of your mind?" Becka asked Jude after they left. "Do you want to get yourself killed?"

"What?" Jude said. "You think I couldn't handle those guys?"

She laughed. "Right, with guns like those . . ."

Jude flexed his biceps. "You kidding me? Sun's out, guns out. I have to register these babies with the FBI," he joked. "These are considered lethal weapons in seventeen states."

Becka shook her head, rang up the next customer, and said, "He was going to squash you like a bug."

"I know," Jude admitted.

"Not very smart, are you?"

"I hoped I could reason with him," Jude explained. "But it was like talking quantum physics with a water buffalo."

She touched Jude's forearm, like a concerned sister. "This is only a summer job. No one expects you to get killed for it."

Jude nodded. "Right, no, right, it was totally dumb. I don't even know what I was thinking. I guess I figured the guys behind the counter would have my back."

"Yeah, sure," she said. "What were they going to do? Throw hand grenades?"

Jude grinned. More customers pressed forward, impatiently waiting. "Thanks," he said. "I guess I owe you."

"Considering I just saved your life? Yeah, I think so," she smiled. "Maybe I'll let you buy me a pretzel someday."

Jude assured Becka that he would. After all, he was already in love with her, and the pretzels were free.

FIVE

Jude stank of hamburger. He could barely stand it: the reek of cooked cow that clung to his clothes on the long bus ride home. He couldn't wait to shower, rejoin the human race.

He saw his father out by the street in a skintight pair of Lycra running shorts, stretching his Achilles tendon with one foot against the curb. Way more of Dad's butt than anybody needed to see.

"Hey, Jude," his father greeted him. "I was just going out for a run. Want to join me?"

He always asked. Jude and his father hadn't run together in years, but he always asked. It was almost sweet. And each time when Jude declined, there was a fleeting look of disappointment in his father's eyes. But there was no way Jude could do it. When it came to running, they were complete opposites.

Jude pulled at the front of his sweat-stained shirt. Shook his head. "I'm covered with grease, can't."

Mr. Fox nodded as if he understood perfectly and checked his sports watch. It was his new toy, a runner's watch with all the latest features, heart-rate monitor, pace alerts, session distance, GPS capability, the works. Jude's father loved data, and as far as Jude was concerned, his father did everything possible to suck the last living ounce of joy out of jogging. Mr. Fox turned something as simple as going for a run into advanced mathematics, measuring every mile, every step, a middle-aged man still chasing his PBT (Personal Best Time). Even so, Jude had to admit it: The guy was in great shape.

"Mom inside?" Jude asked.

"Yes, um, she's upstairs, resting," Mr. Fox answered. "The heat, and—"

"No worries," Jude answered. "I ate at work."

"Oh, that's right. You worked today! How'd it go?"

"Pretty much okay. They gave me a paper hat."

Jude kept the details to the bare minimum. He saw that his father was only half listening. Mr. Fox brought two fingers to his carotid artery, lips moving as he counted the pulse.

"Have a good run," Jude said.

"I'm doing Bender Hill today, five times up, five times down," Mr. Fox announced. "I should be back in roughly sixty-five minutes."

Yeah, roughly. Jude was halfway up the walk and gave no reply. There was never enough light in the house. It could be a beautiful day outside, like today, but you'd never know it. One reason was the overgrown bushes that crowded the front windows and a towering pine that grew too close to the foundation, keeping the home in shade and shadows, its roots causing the front walkway to buckle. When Jude asked his parents why they didn't just cut it down, his father looked away and his mother said the shade helped keep the house cool in the summer. Besides, as she often reminded Jude when she drew the curtains, sunlight faded the carpet.

Jude's mother liked things cool and dark, and had long ago declared war on light itself. She continually snapped down the blinds, pulled closed the curtains, walked around in thin, white sweaters. On good days, Mrs. Fox went to the club for lunch or played tennis with the ladies, lobbing shots from baseline to baseline. But the good days seemed to come less and less. She was a nervous woman who suffered from what she called cluster headaches that forced her to retreat to a darkened bedroom where she lay for long hours at a time. She claimed that sunlight made the headaches worse. Dark and forbidding, it was a house where plants came to wither and die. Jude's father eventually gave up buying Easter lilies or Christmas poinsettias and instead came home one holiday with a large plastic ficus tree. Even his mother's neglect couldn't kill it.

Jude showered and dressed. In the hallway, he paused outside the closed door of his parents' bedroom, tilted an ear, listening for movement.

"Jude?" his mother called.

"Yeah, it's me, Mom," he answered. "How you feeling today?"

A long silence. "I'm sorry, I've got nothing for you in the

kitchen," she finally said, her voice muffled, as if groaned into a pillow.

"That's okay, Mom, I'm good," Jude replied. He considered telling her about work, how some girl saved him from getting pummeled by a trio of behemoths, but it felt awkward trying to talk through a door. He placed his right hand on the door as if to push it open, and he saw his fingers as the legs of a fleshy spider perched there, tingling. Jude rested his head against the jamb, shut his eyes. He waited in the hush for something to happen, some change to occur, but nothing did.

Nothing ever did.

SIX

Corey dropped by around seven. He lived around the corner, and Jude was probably the first friend Corey'd made after moving into the neighborhood. That was almost nine years ago, back in second grade. Corey was one of those guys who couldn't stand sitting around at home; his parents were crazy-strict super-religious types, so he visited other houses and sat around there. Ate their food, too. Jude's parents usually left the boys alone to do as they pleased, so it was a win-win for all concerned.

"Where to?" Jude asked. "Downstairs or . . . ?"

Corey pointed. "Up. Okay?"

They made a short detour into the kitchen where Jude grabbed a bag of pretzels. "Anybody home?" Corey asked.

"They're around somewhere," Jude answered.

Out of long familiarity, Corey led the way up the stairs and into Jude's room. He eased open the second-floor window and climbed out onto the narrow front edge of the roof. Jude followed in bare feet, pretzel bag crinkling. Together they worked their way around to the side of the house, hoisted themselves up like circus performers to the highest point, and perched there like a couple of teenage gargoyles looking down on the neighborhood. Something about that vantage point pleased Corey, soothed him, so Jude never denied his friend that pleasure. Sometimes they'd joke about falling off, daring the other boy to go to the roof's edge, to take a flying leap, but it was only talk. No one ever got close to the upper lip, and no one really wanted to see the other go near it, either.

Though Jude had casual friends and socialized easily in school, there were parts of him that remained fenced off, private places that no one could touch. Corey was the only one Jude allowed inside, the only real friend he had.

Corey was an enthusiastic reader and a nonstop talker. He'd go on jags where he'd read everything by a given author, or anything about a specific topic, until one day he'd announce that he was "full up on it" and had moved on to, say, Stephen King or true-life murders or everything by Max Brooks. Zombies—or Walkers, as he called them—were never far from Corey's mind since, to him, the zombie presence explained everything that was wrong with Long Island.

"Getting near dusk, and the Walkers come out," Corey mused, peering down across the suburban sprawl at neighbors in floppy hats who puttered in gardens, fussing over beds of zinnias and marigolds with pruning shears and watering cans. It was a picture of the American dream, the nice houses and the big cars, but Corey saw something sinister in it, an underlying menace. Jude felt the same way, but for different reasons. Corey Masterson was a misfit in town. He was black in an overwhelmingly white community, and though it rarely ever came up in conversation—why talk about it?—Corey's outsider status was a fact that could not be denied. Jude's sense of alienation was different, harder for him to pinpoint, some inner feeling that he didn't belong to this or any other tribe. Maybe that's what bonded the two boys; they both watched from the fringes with a shared sense of unbelonging.

Corey gestured to where a small group of neighborhood women had gathered. He dabbed a finger at each and said, "Zombie, zombie, zombie."

Jude almost believed it, especially in the case of his next-door neighbor Mrs. Buchman. She was into everyone else's business, always watching, pretending to be friends with anyone who stepped on the sidewalk. "I never liked that woman," he said. "She's into everybody else's shit."

Corey raised an eyebrow at that, the surprising note of anger in Jude's voice, but let it slide. Mrs. Buchman seemed okay to him, for a Walker, with three little blonde daughters, always with a smile on her face. Maybe Jude knew something he didn't.

"Zombies are like terrorist sleeper cells waiting to be activated," Corey continued. "They live here, go about their business—shop, garden, go to PTA meetings—then one day you look up, and they are clawing the eyeballs out of your sockets, gnawing on your bones like you were a rack of baby back ribs!"

Jude lay back, hands behind his head, and watched the sky turn twilight.

"It's easy to fall into their trap," Corey warned. "You look at them and you see a neighbor. The nice ladies who pick up after the dog, smile at the mail carrier, and go to the Y for spin classes. They look at you—and see lunch."

"You watch too much TV."

"Who doesn't?" Corey grinned. "Check out that sweet swimming pool behind Ansari's house, all lit up with floodlights." Corey whistled. "Man, that water is calling my name. We should grab Vinnie and the guys, sneak out, and go pool-hopping some night. I wonder how many we could do. What do you think, Jude, if we swam our way across town? Hopping from pool to pool. That would be a trip."

Jude fell into a brooding silence. He had a history with swimming pools.

Six summers before, Jude's sister Lily drowned in their built-in pool. She was only four years old. There was talk of moving after that, just getting the hell away, but for some reason his parents stayed. Maybe they were frozen in place, stuck there. So they hired an excavation company to fill in the pool. That whole week, Jude watched the men work. They tore at the pool with jackhammers, drilling holes in the bottom, breaking down the sides of the walls. After just one day, it looked like somebody'd bombed the place. The men next appeared with a backhoe, hauling out chunks of concrete. Then came the loads of dirt fill, with a layer of black topsoil for the new garden. Transfixed at an upstairs window, Jude watched the men toil. He felt as if a part of him was interred in that wild torrent of dirt and rubble. And so he buried Lily a second time, and from his window whispered good-bye, lips pressed to the pane.

The next spring his parents labored to transform the scarred earth into a memorial garden. They scratched the dirt and planted shrubs and flowers, a Chinese maple, installed a bench and gravel pathways, but his mother soon lost heart in the project. Over the winter the snow came and most everything died, never to bloom quite the same again. It was supposed to be a garden of tranquility, but in the end the backyard grew into a ramshackle mess of scraggly annuals, a crumbling rock wall, a litter box for neighborhood cats, and weeds, weeds, weeds.

That's the way it was, Jude figured. Everything eventually turned to shit.

Corey read the sullenness in Jude's face and kicked himself for his mistake. Even now, even after all those years. A darkness had descended over Jude. Like that, fast as a finger snap. He was wrapped in it, as if a heavy cloak had fallen around his shoulders.

"What about a movie?" Corey suggested.

"Not tonight," Jude answered.

"Tomorrow night then," Corey persisted. "We'll call the boys. Hang."

"Okay," Jude relented. "Tomorrow."

SEVEN

Jude was back on the grill Sunday, working shoulder to shoulder with the self-proclaimed grillmaster Billy Motchsweller. Jude's glance kept returning to the girl in the middle booth, Becka. She was nice-looking, no doubt about that. Not the sexpot type, not someone who'd cause traffic accidents by walking down the street, but there was something about her that set Becka apart.

"You know her?" Jude asked Billy.

Billy looked up, eyed Becka appraisingly. "Not bad. I'd tap that. She's what we call new talent around here. You like her?"

"Just asking," Jude said.

Billy nodded. "I got a girlfriend at home, man. Four weeks now. I'm faithful, not a player. I come here, do my job, keep my head down, smoke a little weed, and try not to stand around panting like a dog after all these babes in string bikinis that are just *ridonkulous*. I try, I really try. But some days it's *hard.*" He made an obscene gesture. "You know what I'm saying?"

Jude knew what Billy was saying. He would have to be as dumb as a garbage truck to *not* know what Billy was saying; so he made the required response, laughed knowingly. "*Har-har-har.*" Guy talk, just a couple of working stiffs shooting the breeze, pointing and grunting and laughing it out. The kind of conversation most guys felt they were supposed to have as part of the brotherhood of boys: leering, crude, funny, sex-obsessed. It was common ground, like sports talk—"*What about them Yankees?*"—the shared place where guys could meet. We're all a bunch of horndogs, right? Jude wasn't wired like that, but he knew the rules of the game. He was here to work, not make waves; let the pull of the moon take care of the tide.

Besides, it was more disturbing that Billy actually used the word *ridonkulous* in a sentence. That was harder to forgive. You could say it *as a joke*, with lifted eyebrow, but it was another thing altogether to say it straight-faced, like you actually meant it. For the record, Jude felt the same way when people said *ginormous* and *cool beans*. For Jude, it was like watching and enjoying a terrible movie. He loved seeing those movies with Corey, and together they spent giddy hours snorting over the best-worst movies of all time. Classics such as *Roadhouse*, *Anaconda*, *The Beastmaster*, and the all-time best-worst, *Plan 9 from Outer Space*. The thing was, you absolutely had to *know* it was bad—that's what put the *fun* in the *funny*. But if someone like-liked it without irony: Yikes, that was just depressing.

Jude watched as Jessup went out to the cashiers, talking casually with them, full of confidence. Tall, muscular, and handsome, he was the type of all-American hero who could definitely get on a normal, subaverage guy's nerves.

When Kath returned from break, Becka rose to switch places. Jude leaned in for a better look. She was narrow hipped, thin but not frail, about five five. Becka came around the counter, walked past Jude, said something to Roberto that made him laugh, took a bottle of water, lifted a pretzel from the warmer. He watched as she carefully studied the pretzel, sniffed it, dusted off the excess salt, and tore off the tiniest piece imaginable. She was alone in the great wide world with her pretzel, performing some strange ritual, unaware of being watched, cute as all get-go.

He watched her glide into the back room, take off her hat, free that mess of black hair, grab a paperback from her things, and walk out the back door into the sun. When Jessup returned to his back office, Jude went over to Roberto.

He asked about the girl.

"That's Becka McCrystal," Roberto said, sucking down a soft drink. "I kind of know her from school."

"Kind of?"

Roberto shrugged. "We've been in a couple of classes together. We dissected a frog in lab once—she sliced and I diced. It was a bonding experience."

"What else do you know about her?"

Roberto gave him a look. "Who are you, Christopher Columbus? Did you just sail in on the *Mayflower*? You going to stick a flag in her, claim her for King Ferdinand?"

"Dude," Jude said, laughing. "The *Mayflower*? That was the Pilgrims. Plymouth Rock. Columbus drove the *Santa Maria*."

"I thought he rode in on some chick named Nina," Roberto joked, chortling, his big belly shaking with mirth.

"Seriously," Jude persisted. "What's she like?"

Roberto shrugged, made more slurping sounds with his straw. He looked away and said, "She *might* be taken."

"Taken? A boyfriend?"

"No, taken by aliens. She was abducted by little green men last week, they're taking over the planet—or don't you read the *National Star*?" Roberto shook his head, gave Jude a how-dumb-can-you-get? look. Then smiled, just busting. He meant nothing by it. "Yes, Jude, *boyfriend*. An older guy, I think." Roberto may have noticed the look of disappointment on Jude's face, so quickly added, "I don't know for sure. Ask her yourself—she's right out there, see her, sitting on the bench near the flowers."

Jude glanced out the window, saw Becka sitting with one foot tucked under a thigh, nibbling on the pretzel, reading a paperback old-school style.

"So what's up with the supercool manager we were supposed to get?" Jude asked.

"Kenny 'Half-Baked' Mays?" Roberto frowned. "I don't

know what happened. He's not listed on the schedule. I asked Denzel—he says Kenny's filling in over at Zack's Bay."

"How long?"

"Nobody knows," Roberto said.

"That's not good," Jude said.

"Not good? Not good is when an airplane crashes through your roof and lands on your bed like in *Donnie Darko*. And you are sleeping on your bed at the time—*that* is 'not good.' This is worse." Roberto acted it out with his hands, the plane crashing through the roof, the flaming carnage, the whole not goodness of it all.

Jude laughed. He enjoyed talking with Roberto, thinking that maybe they should hang out someday. Besides, it was cool he referenced *Donnie Darko*, a first-rate cult classic. Roberto's mind was alive, full of sudden twists and surprises.

Roberto's eyes grew large. "I got it, the perfect example: The difference between Jessup and Kenny is like the difference between Bert and Ernie."

"From *Sesame Street*?"

"You know another Bert and Ernie?" Roberto asked.

Jude shook his head.

"You have to use your imagination, Lumbus," Roberto said, addressing Jude by his new nickname, short for Columbus, made up on the spot. "Do I have to spell it all out for you? Kenny is Ernie—you want to work for Ernie. He's crazy, he's wild, and his head is orange. Ernie's tight."

"Right," Jude nodded.

"But Bert," Roberto said mournfully, "that's Jessup. We could be in for a long summer."

Jude remembered when he was little, loving Bert's song, "Doin' the Pigeon." He used to dance to it in front of the television. *Whatever happened to that kid?* Jude wondered. *Where'd he go?*

Jude glanced out the window, intrigued by the girl on the bench. Becka McCrystal. She was alone still. But now the book was closed. Her chin lifted to the sun; she looked to the sky, eyes shut, and bathed in its warmth. She appeared perfectly composed and content, like a figure in a painting.

"I'll cover for you," Roberto said. "Go friend her, Lumbus."

Jude ignored the nickname in the hope that, like a stray dog, it might go away if he didn't feed it. "You sure it's okay?" he asked.

"Yeah. Go, man, go," Roberto urged. "Denzel's doing inventory in the back. I'll keep an eye on things. Go click on the *like* button."

reference???

EIGHT

Jude grabbed a broom and dustpan and wandered outside, trying to look his most excellent self while indirectly making his way to where Becka sat, jibing like a sailboat from port to starboard tack. Just a regular guy sweeping up the debris, *hum-dee-dum, dee dum-dum*—no need to get a restraining order. Becka didn't seem to notice his upwind presence, her face still tilted toward the sun.

"You getting your bronze on?" Jude observed. He tried to deliver the line in the least-stalkerlike way possible. He smiled to signal that he was a harmless guy just making conversation.

Becka turned to him, smiled back. "The sun feels so good, especially after being stuck inside all day."

Jude glanced upward, shielding his eyes with the flat of his hand. He gestured to the bench. "Do you mind if I—?"

She slid over to make room.

Jude sat down next to her, picked up the faintest fragrance

off her hair. She smelled fresh, like peaches. All around them, people in bathing suits walked to and from the bathrooms and outdoor showers. They were gorgeous, drunk, fat, sexy, horrifying, freckled, heavily inked, scarred, milky white, sunburned as lobsters, tanned as leather—humanity of every shape and size and shade, but with a lot less clothes than usual. Life's rich pageant.

"So how do you like working the cash register?" Jude said. "It's gotta beat flipping burgers."

"Or working security," Becka said, eyes smiling. "It's okay—boring, I guess. I like watching the people. I give them names, try to imagine their lives."

"What do you mean?"

Becka pointed to a couple holding hands as they walked past. "That guy there, he's, let's see, Dwight. They've been together for two years. He's in construction."

"Nah," Jude said. "See that tattoo on his biceps? 'Semper fi.' That's the Marine motto, *always faithful.* He just got back from the Middle East."

Becka's eyes widened. "And she's been cheating on him!"

Jude laughed. "My name's Jude."

"Oh, like the song?"

The boy nodded; he'd heard that one a lot. It usually irritated him, but not coming from her lips. "My mother used to be a Beatles freak," he explained, "so I guess I'm supposed to be the guy in the song."

"What does he *do* in the song?" Becka asked. There was a

flicker in her eyes, a dance of light, as if she already knew the answer.

Jude looked away, uncomfortable. *He makes it better*, he thought. *He goes out and gets her.* But Jude did not say the words.

"I'm Becka Bliss McCrystal." She reached out her hand for an official handshake. She had a firm grip and looked him square in the eyes.

He saw that her clear eyes were green, as if an artist had painted them while dreaming of the Mediterranean Sea. And then the word came to him: *turquoise.* "Bliss, I like that," Jude said.

A chiseled bodybuilder, overcooked by the sun, paraded past in a minuscule bathing suit.

"Holy God, look at the size of that guy," Becka said.

"I'm guessing he works out," Jude noted.

"In front of a mirror, all day long," Becka said. "Exhibition-ist. Not my type."

"Oh?" Jude asked. "You have a type?"

Becka turned to look at him, a crooked smile on her face. "I don't know yet. I'm not really all that into looks." She paused. "I'll know it when I meet him. What about you? Do you have a girlfriend?"

"Me?" Jude felt suddenly tongue-tied, alarmed by Becka's directness, not sure how the conversation had so quickly turned intimate. "No, I'm basically solo."

Becka laughed at that. "Yeah, who needs the old ball and chain, is that how it is?"

"No, I guess, I don't know, maybe I'm like you. I'll know when I meet her," and he resisted adding, *and I'm looking right at her.*

"I crushed on a guy for a long time but finally realized it was hopeless," Becka confided. She glanced toward the ocean for an answer, then gestured with her bottle of water toward the building. "Looks like somebody wants you," she said. There behind the wall-length glass window stood his boss. Denzel Jessup had a clipboard tucked under his left arm and with his right fist knocked on the window to get Jude's attention. He did not look happy.

Busted.

"Ooooh, you're in trouble," Becka half sang, drawing out the vowels in *trouble.*

Jude cast a worried look at Becka. "You think I'm fired?"

"Meh," she replied with a shrug. "I doubt it. How many people are dumb enough to work here in the first place?"

Jude headed back to the building, walking quickly. He paused to pick up a phantom paper with his broom and dustpan, trying to make the ruse look good.

"Hey, Jude," she called after him.

He stopped, turned. "Yeah?"

"At least you're still wearing your hat—that's gotta be worth something," she said, cheerfully patting her own head.

Jude reached for his head, felt the hat perched there like an awkward duck. He'd forgotten all about it. A warm rush of blood came to his cheeks. He must've looked very smooth, chatting up Becka with a paper hat on his head.

Of course, Jessup didn't buy Jude's story about cleaning up outside—as if Jude was suddenly possessed with this tremendous desire to pick up litter. Yeah, right.

"You can't just decide to take a break whenever you want," Jessup told Jude. "That's not how the job works."

"It was slow, I thought that—"

"You 'thought'?" Jessup echoed. "Mr. Fox, let me tell you this right now. Thinking is not your job."

Jude nodded, absorbing the insult.

"There's always something to do around here," Jessup continued. "If it's slow, you can wipe down the counter, replenish the stock, organize the inventory, sweep out the supply closet. The important thing is, *look busy*. If you can't think of something to do, I'll think of it for you. And believe me, you won't like the kind of jobs that I'll think up." He smiled. "And guess what?"

"What?"

"I just thought of a good one," Jessup said, teeth gleaming. "Follow me."

Jessup went into the back, dug around in a deep-bottomed desk drawer, and pulled out a metal scraper. "Grab a bucket from the supply closet and come with me."

The counter crew watched, grinning behind Jessup's back. Roberto had his hands out, palm up, wearing a wha'-happened? expression, as if it wasn't his idea in the first place.

Jessup stopped at the outdoor picnic area. He asked, "Have you ever been to Disneyland?"

"Once, a long time ago," Jude answered. He remembered that trip to Disney; it was burned inside his memory. He pictured himself waiting impatiently while his little sister Lil stood on line to meet the pretty princesses. He could see her in his mind's eye, golden-haired, bouncing on her toes with excitement, clutching an autograph book to her chest. It was their last summer together.

Jude looked at Jessup, blinked, said, "I was too young; I don't remember much."

"They hate gum at Disney, did you know that?"

"No, I wasn't aware how they felt about gum," Jude replied. He didn't like where this was going.

"Do you know you can't buy a stick of gum in the entire park? They refuse to sell it," Jessup said. "They treat gum like it's crack cocaine."

Jude eyed the scraper in Jessup's hand. The bucket. All those yellow plastic tables in the eating area. Must have been fifteen tables, easy.

"You know why, don't you?" Jessup asked.

"I've got a pretty good idea," Jude said.

"Tell me."

Jude sighed. It was almost funny, discussing Disneyland's policy on chewing gum. "The kids stick the gum on stuff," he ventured.

Jessup clapped his hands once, pleased. "Exactly right, Mr. Fox! The gum goes everywhere—on the sidewalks, under chairs and tables, on the rides, you name it. That's what people do with gum—they don't care, they stick it anywhere. So the accountants at Disney sat down and did a cost analysis. Do you know what that is?"

"They, uh . . ." Jude was getting tired of this game. He was ready to serve his punishment. "No, what's it mean?"

"They figured out how much money they'd earn by selling gum. Then they figured out how much it would cost to clean up after it," Jessup explained. "They realized it would cost more than they'd earn. It wasn't worth the hassle. The solution: Ban gum from the park!"

"Pretty smart rat, that Mickey Mouse," Jude said.

Jessup handed the scraper to Jude, gestured to the tables. "Unfortunately, this isn't Disney. You work at West End Two—for today, at least. I suggest you start scraping."

The honest truth? It wasn't that bad. Jude was outside in the fresh air, even if he spent most of it on his back, or crunched up in a contorted knot under the table like some kind of yoga master. His arms ached after a while, his fingers stiffened; he switched hands every few minutes. Even so, Jude didn't mind being alone with his thoughts. From under the table, he was like a mechanic under a car—invisible to most of the people

54

around him. *Unseen.* Besides, it offered a provocative vantage point on the girls as they walked past.

Jude didn't love that he got himself into Jessup's doghouse on his second day on the job. Not a great start. He couldn't wait; nope, he had to listen to Roberto, go outside to meet that girl. Becka Bliss McCrystal. And all he could think was this: *She was totally worth it.* Jude pictured her thick black hair, her dark eyebrows and easy smile. The way she sat with her spine perfectly straight, relaxed but elegant. He wondered if she was a dancer. And wondered also how he could describe her to Corey, who'd be eager to hear all about it. He might as well try to describe the way a breeze comes off the ocean or the way the air smells after a morning rain.

West End Two attracted people with cars. There was no way to get there without your own wheels, no bus service to that part of the park, and the central boardwalk didn't extend that far west. Because it was the closest beach to the city, West End Two drew a multicultural, slightly older, urban-flavored crowd. And because the parking lot was so far from the waterline, not many families came, either. The crowd was almost exclusively ages sixteen to twenty-five, with some of the most beautiful girls Jude had ever seen in one place. He could already tell this job was going to be an exquisite form of torture.

All he could think of was one girl in particular, a face he barely knew.

Near the end of day, after he scraped tables for an hour at least, the muscles in Jude's forearms burned. He felt a crick in his neck, so he stood to stretch. Jude noticed a little girl walk past, comically trying to balance a soda and a container of fries. A smattering of fries spilled onto the sand after her, like Gretel's trail of crumbs in the woods. Ahead of her walked an older boy, surely her brother; he had the same body type and tussled blond hair, not much different from his own. Jude guessed the boy was about twelve years old. He stood watching as they walked in the sand toward the water, searching for a familiar blanket or beach umbrella.

Just a boy and a boy's sister.

Take her hand, Jude silently urged the boy. *Don't let her out of your sight.* But the older boy kept walking, confident that his sister would always be there. Jude felt an old hollowness return to his stomach. He watched until they disappeared into the horizon, smaller and smaller, and then, fully gone, swallowed up by sand and sky.

Bickering seagulls landed to scavenge the dropped fries, Gretel's trail vanishing to nothingness as they ate until there was no trace of the girl's passage except for her small footsteps in the sand.

NINE

It was finals week at school, so Jude spent late nights cramming for tests. Still, he rose early most mornings to run, hard and long, just to clear his head. Jude sometimes imagined himself as an ancient Navajo among the mesas, running till he found the next tribe somewhere over the rise. It was never about numbers for Jude. Not the distance traveled, nor the time it took. He ran for the love of running, like a colt in the grass. All the while, Becka on his mind.

Come the weekend, he looked forward to work. Jessup said he wouldn't put Jude on a full-time schedule until school ended in another week. But on Saturday the overcast sky darkened as the hours passed, and it became obvious that it would be a disappointing day for sun worshippers. The concession was overstaffed, the crowds meager, nothing to do. Jessup went around tapping people on the shoulder, sending them home.

Becka wasn't too happy about it. She'd only worked three

hours. "Well, I guess I'm outta here," she told Jude. Her eyes spoke for a moment, lingered on his for an extra beat, and he sensed she was waiting for something.

"Hey, um," he said, holding her there, "maybe I could get a ride from you. I mean, would that be okay?"

Gladness flickered on Becka's face, like wind in the trees. She smiled and said yes.

"Problem is, I'm not off yet," Jude said, trying not to sound too eager.

"You could ask him," Becka suggested. "See if he'll let you go."

"I could use the money," Jude countered.

Becka shrugged, noncommittal. "Up to you. Either way, I'm leaving in five minutes."

Jessup hemmed and hawed at Jude's request, said he was letting most of the cashiers go but still needed a few good workers for closing. Jude was persuasive; Denzel finally told him to go before he changed his mind.

Being alone with Becka outside of work made Jude feel light-headed, like he was walking on soft, fluffy clouds. Becka shifted around a bunch of junk in her car—it was a mess with blankets, bags, books, CDs, magazines, assorted crap everywhere—to make room for Jude in the front.

"What can I say? I'm a slob," Becka said without apology.

The car was an old Toyota, a little worse for wear. "Sweet ride," Jude whistled.

"You can walk if you'd like," Becka replied. She grabbed a

canvas bag from the backseat and said she'd be right back. "I've got to get out of these clothes."

She returned with her hair tied loosely back, wearing shorts and some kind of spaghetti-strap top. She looked great, with tanned, toned legs. "I feel better already," Becka announced, turning the key. "Now I'm myself." She found a song on the radio and turned it up loud, moving her head to the beat. Becka was transformed, and it wasn't just the clothes. She seemed more playful out in the real world, quicker to smile, more fun, way sexier. As they drove east toward the round-about, Becka asked, "Are you in a hurry to get home?"

Jude told her that he definitely was not.

Becka pulled the car into the huge Field Four parking lot. "Let's do the boardwalk," she said.

"Do you play putt-putt?" Jude asked.

"I'm beast!" Becka said. "You are so dead."

"Oh, really?" Jude asked skeptically.

Becka nodded. "When it comes to putt-putt, I'm pretty much a ninja."

Jude laughed, pushing her gently on the shoulder. "Ninja, huh? We'll see about that."

Jones Beach had a two-mile boardwalk, with the sand and the Atlantic to the south, and various concessions, pools, and sport activities on the other side. There was shuffleboard, tennis, basketball, and more. Like the boardwalk itself, most of the courts were in a semi-dilapidated condition. The entire place had seen better days, including the ocean itself. Yet on sizzling summer afternoons, the whole place jumped. Not today though, when it felt like the park had been built expressly for Jude and Becka's pleasure.

"It's quiet," Jude observed. "I like it."

"Look at that surf," Becka said, marveling at the ocean. "The waves are kicking up pretty high. Storm's coming."

"I wish I didn't feel like such a dork in this uniform," Jude said.

"So take off your shirt."

Jude had spent a lot of time over the past few years at the beach. It was no big deal for him to hang out all day in bathing trunks, shirtless. He had a firm stomach, did push-ups, looked okay—nothing to be ashamed about. But this felt different, alone with Becka. He rolled his shirt sleeves above his shoulders and left it at that.

At the third hole of the putt-putt course, as Jude struggled to direct his ball safely through a rotating windmill, he asked Becka why she decided to work at Jones Beach instead of some other job.

Becka balanced the putter upright in her palm, making small adjustments to keep it from falling. "My older brothers worked here, so did a lot of their friends," she said. "I guess it felt like an easy job." She popped the club into the air, spun around, and caught it with her right hand.

"What's the matter, no jobs at the circus?" Jude joked.

"I wish! You should see me on a unicycle," Becka said. "Do you want to know *why* I'm working?"

Jude ventured a guess. "You love the smell of sunscreen and grease?"

"Yeah, sure, who doesn't?" Becka replied. "Actually, I'm saving for my dream guitar."

"Really, you play?"

"Since I was twelve. I love it."

"Me, too," Jude said. "What kind of guitar do you want to buy?"

"Rickenbacker 330," Becka answered.

"You like that jangle sound, huh?"

"John Lennon, Johnny Marr, Peter Buck, they all played Rickenbackers," Becka said. "You know Guitar World in Massapequa? That's where I'm going to buy it. I've got mine all picked out."

"Tell me," Jude said, tapping the ball into the hole. He didn't bother to fill in the scorecard. Jude hated those ultra-competitive guys who took things like P.E. way too seriously. He and Becka randomly cut over from the third to the eleventh hole. Nobody was around, nobody cared, and this one had a fake pirate ship in the middle of it to enhance the awesomeness.

"You should see it, gorgeous guitar," Becka enthused. "Semi-hollow maple body, fireglo finish, rosewood fretboard with dot inlays, single-coil pickups—"

"Wow, you know your stuff," Jude said. "That's not a cheap guitar."

"Almost two thousand balloons," Becka said. "My parents are willing to go halfsies."

"Halfsies?" Jude laughed.

"You know what I mean," Becka protested, a hint of color rising to her cheeks. "I've been staring at that guitar for the past year. It's my goal for this summer. I need that guitar."

Jude knew exactly how she felt. He was always coveting a new guitar, or considering a trade-in. Every guitar had an individual sound, a character of its own, something that most people didn't understand. Jude and Becka talked guitars and music, compared iPods and favorite tunes, thrilled to have that connection. "I'd love to hear you play," Jude said.

"I sometimes jam out with my brothers and their friends, nothing serious, just goofin' in the garage," Becka said. "You should come over someday."

"You've never even heard me play," Jude said.

"I can tell about these things—it's part of my ninja powers. I know you're good," Becka replied. Teeing off, she swung mightily and bounced the green ball off the turf and into a bush.

"Nice shot, tiger," Jude chided. "I hate to say this, but for a ninja you're kind of hopeless. Me, I'm more like Chuck Norris. Last time I played an eighteen-hole golf course, I scored a twelve—two off my personal best."

Becka laughed, said, "Chuck Norris doesn't bowl strikes; he knocks down one pin and the other nine faint."

For the next few holes, Becka surprised him with her knowledge of cornball Chuck Norris jokes. "I learned them from my brother Matt," Becka explained. "He's a pop-culture killer—he'll run a joke into the ground till it's good and dead."

This girl was cool, Jude thought—like a guy. If it turned out Becka liked chicken wings and college basketball, he'd drop down on his knees to propose.

And at that, the sky cracked open. The rain that had threatened all day finally came, in torrents, soaking them instantly. Jude and Becka ditched their clubs on the spot, ran hard toward the car, pausing in the shelter of an echoing underpass. They laughed together, shivering close, while the rain drummed overhead.

Becka had a towel in her car and dried off. She even tried to lend him a Batgirl T-shirt, but Jude couldn't see himself in it. "I'd rather die of hypothermia," he explained. Becka shrugged and drove to Jude's house, door-to-door service. "Here you go," she announced, pulling over to the curb.

"Thanks, Beck," he said, and paused. "I really had a great time."

"Me too." She smiled at him, studied his house from the road. "This isn't too far from where I live, you know. I'm just on the other side of the Seaford-Oyster Bay Expressway."

Jude waited, not ready to leave the car. It was still raining pretty hard. Becka flicked off the wipers, let the water stream over the windshield. The windows clouded, closed in on them like a canopy bed.

Becka looked toward the house. "I hate to say this, but that is one sorry-looking tree you have in front of your house."

She wasn't the first one to make that observation.

"I know," Jude said. "My mother likes it, though. She calls it her giant parasol, keeping out the sun and rain."

Becka shook her head. "Nothing can stop the rain."

Jude nodded, lips downturned. "You have plans for tonight?"

For the flash of an instant, Becka looked distressed. Then recovered, said, "Yeah, kind of do. You?"

Jude shrugged. "Probably the same old thing—another Saturday-night brodown."

Becka laughed. "A brodown, huh? Sounds fierce. What do you boys do? Play video games and burp a lot?"

"Something like that," Jude said. "If you fart, nobody has to apologize. That's how we roll. Seriously, we won't go big. I have to be at work by nine tomorrow."

"Really? Same here."

"I'll see you then." Jude lifted the handle, cracked the door.

"You don't have your license yet, do you?"

Jude shook his head. "I was thinking about running to work tomorrow."

"Running? Like with your actual feet?" Becka asked.

Jude grinned. "It's not that far, probably take me an hour. I can shower and change when I get there. Jessup let me stash a spare set of clothes in his office."

Becka's head ducked forward, shock registered on her face. "Really? Won't you be exhausted?"

"I love running," Jude answered. "It beats waiting for the bus."

"Are you some kind of track star?"

"Used to be," Jude admitted, "but I quit. I guess I'm not a team guy. The coach was super-serious." Jude remembered the pressure, the high expectations everyone had of him. As a ninth grader, Jude almost beat the school record in the mile. He was shocked at that, because he wasn't even really trying. After he pulled in that time, things changed. Everyone's eyes were on him, watching, watching. So he ditched. "I just love to run," he tried to explain to Becka. "It doesn't matter to me how long it takes. I'm not trying to beat anybody. I don't want to be the star."

Becka listened with interest. That was her gift, Jude realized: She had a way of making him open up about stuff he rarely talked about.

"I could give you a ride . . . if you want," Becka offered.

"Okay, you sure? I'd like that," Jude said. "I'll be ready at, um, what time?"

"I'll text you." So they did the phone swap thing, punching in the numbers, before saying good-bye.

Jude ran into the house, darting between raindrops. *Becka Bliss McCrystal*, he thought.

Becka, Becka, Becka.

By the time he reached his bedroom, there was already a message on his cell. It was from Becka: *Hey u! Now what r u doing?*

TEN

That night, Jude told Corey Man about his rainy afternoon with Becka and the message she'd left on his cell. "What did she mean, ya think?" Jude asked.

Corey was sprawled on the bedroom floor, Jude's acoustic guitar in his hands, strumming artlessly. Corey couldn't play except for three simple chords, but he loved holding Jude's guitar, striking hilarious rock star poses. Corey shrugged. "She likes you, I guess."

"Yeah, but—"

"Lemme see, lemme see," Corey said, indicating the phone. He tapped some buttons and parsed the message. He pointed to the screen, *hmmmmmed* thoughtfully. "You didn't tell me about the first part, where she started with 'Hey, you.' That's promising, Jude."

"'Hey, you'? That's a good sign?"

Corey shook his head definitively. "Do I have to explain everything? 'Hey, you'—that means she's way, way into you. I mean, if she wrote 'Hi,' you might as well give it up. Forget it, you'd be done. 'What's up?' that means she's like a buddy," he opined. "And I have to say, I like that she doesn't have emoticons sprinkled all over the place; that shit's annoying."

Jude could almost see the logic behind Corey's analysis.

Corey continued: "This here, where she asks, 'Now what are you doing?' That means she can't stop thinking about you." He handed the cell back to Jude. "You're on her mind, Jude. The girl's obviously obsessed. Only danger is, she might be a stage-five clinger."

"I hate that about girls," Jude countered. "Everything's in code. They never say what they mean."

"True," Corey said. "But you have to remember, they are not of this planet. She's using a secret language. It's what girls do."

"When I asked her what she was doing tonight, she got this weird look on her face," Jude confided.

"Hmmmm," Corey murmured. "That's not good. What did she say exactly?"

"She 'kind of' had plans," Jude recalled, placing air quotes around the key words.

"Oh, I got it," Corey said, stomping his feet and laughing. "She's got a boyfriend!"

"You think?"

"Oh, yeah, no doubt," Corey teased. "I've seen this movie before, and believe me, Jude, she's got a guy stashed away somewhere."

Jude prodded at Corey with his foot, a little annoyed by him. He decided against mentioning that Becka herself had already admitted to "crushing on some guy"—her words, not his. Maybe it was a problem, maybe not. Corey didn't know Becka. Hell, Jude hardly knew her.

"She might be in transition," Corey mused.

"What?"

"Maybe she's open to change," Corey said. "I don't know, I'm not the love doctor. We better get over to the Stallion's house. He said Lee'll pick us up over there."

"Lee has his mother's car," Jude complained. "Why can't he swing by here to pick us up?"

"He's power trippin'," Corey explained. "It's no big deal. We'll be there in five minutes on our bikes."

"It's not raining anymore," Jude said. "Let's walk."

"That's what I said," Corey agreed.

Vinnie Canino was the next member in Jude's inner circle. The boys started calling him Stallion after Corey saw the movie *Rocky*. So Vinnie Canino became the Italian Stallion. The name, shortened to Stallion, stuck as an affectionate epithet between friends; it never went viral. To the rest of the high school, he was simply Canino, or Vinnie C.—always Vinnie, never Vin or Vincent.

Teenage boys are rarely exactly like their fathers. They say the acorn never falls far from the tree—but sometimes it bounces, rolls down a hill, and strays as far from that tree as acornly possible. Especially if it's a teenage acorn and Dad's a dud. Few sixteen-year-olds wanted to hear they were just like their fathers, including Vinnie Canino. Except in Vinnie's case, it was so totally true. He was a younger version of his old man, spit out by the Master of the Universe's awesome copy machine. A mini-me. A clone. A glance at Mr. Canino revealed Vinnie's fate. So the best way to describe Vinnie would be to walk up to his house, ding-dong the doorbell, and hope his father might answer.

"Hey, hey, how ya boys doin' tonight? Stopped rainin', huh?" Mr. Canino said now, peeking his head out the door, breathing it all in. "Will ya look at those clouds. Beautiful. Am I right or am I wrong?" It was a rhetorical question. Mr. Canino knew he was right; it was never in doubt. He had that confidence all fathers had, whether they had any brains or not.

Mr. Stanley Canino was short and solid, an Italian fire hydrant. He wore expensive pressed jeans, a perpetual tan, and a black satin button-down shirt like a Vegas entertainer. Squiggly chest hairs tried to climb out of the shirt. His black hair was pulled back into an exceedingly tight ponytail, which set Mr. Canino apart from his neighbors, who did not wear ponytails. On weekends he moonlighted as a drummer in a wedding band, playing all the hits from the seventies, eighties, nineties, and aughties. He was a grown-up Romeo, and his lovely wife, Melinda, had benefited from obvious surgical enhancements that had puffed and pulled and plumped things to alarming dimensions. Something about her face seemed off. Vinnie's mom was at war against both time and gravity, urged on, no doubt, by Stanley Canino's hirsute zeal and open checkbook.

"Vinnie's up in his room—you know the way, boys. Come on inside; you're lettin' the bugs in." He smiled brightly, if distractedly, and spoke in a rapid-fire rhythm. Mr. Canino liked Jude and had even jammed with him a few times on old classics like "Bell Bottom Blues" and "Little Wing." He often pushed CDs into Jude's hands, sometimes even breaking out the vinyl. Even so, Mr. Canino laughed most with Corey, going down in the boxer's crouch, the whole buddy-buddy routine. It was a fact. Everybody's parents loved Corey; he had a natural way of saying the things that parents liked to hear. Not phony, either. Without effort, Corey made people happy.

The boys knew to slip off their shoes upon entering; it was that kind of house, and the Caninos were that kind of family. The furnishings were ornate and stunningly ugly. Lots of brass—everything seemed to shine—and no chair looked like it would be comfortable to sit on.

Vinnie was in his room, blasting rap, doing curls with forty-pound dumbbells, alternating with sets of push-ups. He was shirtless and glistening, the room smelling of stifled air and sweat. There was a full-length mirror on the closet door that got plenty of use.

Vinnie was upbeat.

"Hell, yeah, I'm ready to go out," he told the boys. "I'm up for anything, why the hell not? Let's lock and load and burn this damn town *down.*"

Not in those words exactly, but that was the prevailing Canino sentiment. Vinnie approached life like a Labrador puppy. He was bounding, enthusiastic, flowing with excess energy, good-natured, and often clumsy. Though Vinnie wasn't a natural fit with Jude and Corey, in real life these kinds of accidental friendships happened all the time. Sometimes the people you hung out with were just old habits, like the worn pathways of shortcuts to school. People got comfortable with each other, tolerant, and accepting. Vinnie was a nice guy and good for a laugh. The Stallion always had money and, like his friends, hadn't yet found a better way to spend the days and nights—though he was working on it, pretty much full time. Like a fisherman on a pier, Vinnie forever angled for some girl's affections. That was usually the first question out of Vinnie's mouth. "Where the girls at tonight? Any parties? Anything going on?"

The Stallion knew the answers would be dismal—the basic info had already been texted and digested—but that was Vinnie, ever the optimist. He was preternaturally on the prowl. There was a girl out there somewhere in the sea, maybe an acrobat or an escapee from some carnival eager to perform unspeakable acts. It was only a matter of putting out the right bait and reeling her home.

Stallion took a quick shower, shaved, splashed on cologne (chum for the ladies!), and was ready by the time Lee, a red-haired senior, showed up in his mother's Explorer. He pulled alongside the curb and honked.

Stallion charged out the front door and called, "Shotgun, no blitz!"

Corey and Jude never had a chance. When it came to calling shotgun—the right to sit in the front passenger seat—the Stallion was the fastest draw in the East. By adding "no blitz," Vinnie protected his claim from the dreaded "blitz attack," when another passenger could still run ahead to reach the passenger door first. The boys followed the official rules of shotgun, a strict set of guidelines that were accepted as if Moses himself had carried them down from the mountaintop on stone tablets. Even amateurs knew that if you yelled "Shotgun!" you got to ride in the front seat. But there existed several complex clauses and loopholes. For example, shotgun could not be called in advance or from indoors or if the caller was not wearing shoes. The boys knew this as "the Canino Addendum," a rule instituted after barefoot Vinnie had run outside while his guests slipped on their sneakers by the front door. A driver's girlfriend was not required to call shotgun; it was assumed. And so on.

Safely ensconced in the shotgun seat, Vinnie patted his pockets. "Hold up, I forgot my wallet," he grumbled. Vinnie realized he was in peril of breaking the reentry rule, which stated that a passenger surrenders shotgun status if he goes back inside for any reason. Resigned to his fate, a downcast Stallion headed back into the house while his thick cologne formed a trail behind him, streaming off his head like the pillowy exhaust from a jet.

By the time Vinnie returned, Corey had positioned himself in the front seat. From the back, Jude had barely noticed. He'd just received another text from Becka.

I just got my hand stuck in a can of Pringles!

ELEVEN

"I talked to the Duffmeister today," Vinnie announced from the backseat. "He's a hurting unit." Vinnie was referring, of course, to their friend Terry O'Duffigan, aka the Duffmeister. According to Vinnie, Terry had gotten his hands on a bottle of vodka the previous night and had attempted to drown himself with it. Turned out to be a bad idea.

The big problem with drinking, Jude believed, was drunk people. They usually acted like idiots. At parties or in the woods with friends, Jude always stayed in control. The Duffmeister was something else entirely. He changed personalities. After a couple of beers, Terry became an outsize version of himself—louder, funnier, happier—until he passed out or threw up. But it never seemed to faze him. Terry liked drinking, maybe too much. Some guys were like that. Girls too.

"Amateur," Lee scoffed.

Vinnie laughed. "He was up all night, calling Ralph on the big white telephone!"

That got a laugh from everyone. The Duffmeister would be hearing about it for weeks.

"Did he get caught?" Corey asked.

"What do you think?" Vinnie answered. "He was hacking into the toilet bowl. Those things echo! 'Help me, heeelllp me!'" Vinnie whined in a slurry voice. "Duff's parents were cool about it, but he decided to lie low tonight."

Jude tapped a message into his cell: *Drivin around. Bored. U?*

The boys were not big partiers. In fact, as a loose group, they could more easily be identified by what they were *not* rather than what they were. Not geeks, not freaks, not burn-outs. In that sense they were like the color black, actually an *absence* of color, defined by what it was not: not blue, red, orange, green, heliotrope, or puce. On aimless nights like to-night, when they had no fixed plan other than to "get out," Lee often grew irritable. He steered his mother's car down different roads, pulled into fast-food places so they could buy fries and shakes, or on warm nights lean against the bike racks like a shaggy band of brothers, harmless outcasts in basketball kicks, before shoving off again to specifically elsewhere.

Lee pulled the Ford to the curb. He demanded, "Where now, geniuses?"

Shrugs, silence all around.

"I am *not* going to drive around all night if there's no-freakin'-where to go. It's stupid and I'm sick of it."

The guys knew it was all bluff. Lee loved sitting behind that wheel; he just liked complaining about it *almost* as much. As

the oldest among them—Lee would be a senior next year—
he held a status and a power that made him the King of Saturday Nights. He wasn't about to surrender his only true
advantage. He snapped, "Gas costs money, you know."

Yup, *yawn*, they knew. So they dug into their pockets, pulled
out slim wallets or crumpled bills, pooled their resources, and
handed up twelve bucks worth of good times on the asphalt
wonderways. Freedom to burn.

"Okay, great," Lee muttered, organizing and refolding the
cash. On principle, he refused to chip in. And what could anyone say to that? He asked again: "Where now?"

It was the conversation Jude dreaded. The "What do you
wanna do now?" routine. For days and weeks, months and
years they batted the same words back and forth. *What do
you want to do? I don't know: What do you want to do?* It made
Jude's ears ring, a big heavy bell clanging inside his skull.
Here they were, done with finals, with nowhere to go. Jude felt
trapped in the soft, cushioned boredom of suburban life. Maybe
a good place to grow up, and maybe okay for settling down,
but Jude was in neither of those places. He was in between, a
lit fuse, a teenage rocket exploding, and he felt there was
nothing for him on this Wrong Island.

They ran through the usual list of options: the beach, the
woods behind the high school, Canino's basement, Mill Pond,
the bowling alley, and on and on. One by one, the ideas were
shot down before they could even take wing, like slaughtered
ducks on a lake, blood and feathers everywhere.

Jude half considered bagging out altogether—go home and play guitar, watch TV. But he'd take too much crap for bailing now.

"How about the Amityville Horror House?" Corey suggested—fascinated as he was by close encounters with the paranormal. So off the boys went, relieved to have a destination. It was the crucial distinction between wandering around all night like four lost losers or having a purpose. To everyone's surprise, a squirming Vinnie produced a slim bottle of brown liquid from deep in the nether regions of his jeans.

"Sweet, where'd that come from?" Lee asked.

"Uranus, I think," Corey commented, frowning.

Vinnie grinned. "I raided my father's liquor cabinet. He gets bottles all the time as holiday gifts. He'll never miss it."

Vinnie unscrewed the cap and gave the bottle a sniff. "Bourbon, boys. Bottoms up!" He lifted the liquor to his lips and slugged down a shot.

"Save some for the rest of us," Lee complained. "Pass that bad boy up front."

"Lee—" Corey chided.

"What? You want to get out and walk?" Lee countered, snatching at the bottle. "I'm going to take a sip, that's all. Since when did you join Mothers Against Drunk Driving?"

Lee offered the drink to Jude, who declined. "Nah, I'm good."

"Oh, that's right, you like the runner's high," Vinnie teased. "Is it really true, though? After a long run, do you feel all tripped out?"

Jude shrugged.

"The runner's high," Lee scoffed. "If I run around the block, all I want to do is throw up a lung."

The boys drove in silence, lulled by the hum and thrum of rubber on asphalt, the headlights mystical on the wet, shimmering road, content to be headed somewhere. The Amityville house was a place to go, another bullet to kill Saturday night.

Jude couldn't imagine stealing alcohol from his father. The guy was Mr. Free Range Organic, constantly shoving bananas in the blender, spooning in heaps of protein mix, talking about roughage and—worst of all—his weekly acai colon cleanse. Mr. Fox counted his calories, monitored his cholesterol levels, and shuddered at the thought of an ice cream sundae. His father drinking bourbon? Jude couldn't see it.

As for his mom, she practically had a pharmacy in the medicine cabinet—Jude had snooped it out like Encyclopedia Brown—with little bottles of Vicodin and OxyContin to kill the pain and who knows what else? The delicate chemistry of happiness. At least she didn't drink anymore. It was something.

Lee took another short sip, passed it along like a big shot. Jude tried not to judge. He guessed everybody had their own way of keeping the wolves at bay.

"What'd you do last night, Corey Man?" Canino asked.

"Not much," Corey said. "Some powerdisking. I caught up on the final season of *Friday Night Lights.* Why didn't anybody tell me that show jumped the shark? There's not enough football. Then I finished reading *Breakfast of Champions.* Insane and hilarious."

"Reading's bad for the eyes," Canino noted. "You'll go blind that way."

"Thank you, Mr. Twenty-Twenty," Corey retorted.

"*Breakfast of Champions*? What is it about, Wheaties?" Lee joked. He laughed after delivering the line, like the canned soundtrack on TV sitcoms: "Ha-ha-ha." It wasn't that funny.

"Yeah, right, barfwad. I read a book about a box of cereal," Corey scoffed. "Seriously, Kurt Vonnegut was totally righteous. He looked around at all the stupidity in the world and pointed out how dumb everything was—and he was funny as hell doing it too."

"Yeah, like what's so stupid?" Lee asked, as if he didn't like the sound of this Vonnegut guy.

"Like 'The Star-Spangled Banner,' for instance."

"He thinks it's stupid? Our national anthem?" Lee was gearing up into argument mode.

Jude groaned internally. Lee was becoming a problem. Car or no car, he was growing tiresome. Something had to change. Jude couldn't wait to get his license. *Freedom.*

"Admit it, Lee, it's a lousy-sounding song," Corey replied. "Vonnegut says it's gibberish sprinkled with question marks. . . . 'Oh, say, can you see . . . ?'"

"What does he want? The song is about a battle—'rockets' red glare'!"

"'The bombs bursting in air,'" Jude added.

"Exactly," Corey said, rising to the challenge. "What kind of country picks that as their song? I mean, look at us. We didn't pick it, we're stuck with it—just like everything else around here."

We didn't start the fire, Jude thought.

"Maybe we should all vote on our favorite song?" Lee asked.

"Yeah, that'd be great," Jude commented. "Make it a popularity contest. The new national anthem would be sung by the latest Disney teen product or, like, Lady Gaga."

"Skank," Vinnie opined.

"She's hot," Lee said. "I'd do her."

Jude frowned. "*You'd do her.* That'll be the day. Do you ever wonder if she'd do you?" He made no attempt to hide the irritation in his voice. Lee danced on his nerves.

"I don't know what the hell she'd do," Lee snapped back, glaring at Jude in the rearview mirror. "Don't get political on me, Jude. I'm just stating my personal policy on who'd I'd be willing to bang."

Vinnie snorted. "Right, and Lee's got such high standards."

"She's gotta have two legs and a pulse!" Corey exclaimed, finger thrust into the air—and even Lee had to laugh at that.

"I'm not one of those necrophiliacs," Lee said. "No corpses, no circus freaks, no carny tang, that's where I draw the line."

"Carny tang? What the hell?" Jude laughed.

Meanwhile, Vinnie eyed the road. Their car was stuck behind a slow, gray Impala. "Come on, Lee," he urged. "Pass this old lady."

Lee hit the turn signal, announced "Turbo jets on," and accelerated into the left lane.

"Slinggg-shot!" Vinnie cried, as the car sped past the chugging Impala.

Corey returned to the main topic. He couldn't help himself. He was one of those guys who became like a missionary knocking on doors, spreading the good word about his latest discoveries. It could be a new song or a pretty girl or a phone app or the coming zombie apocalypse. Corey was like a bull rider who couldn't let go. "It's what the song's *about*, Lee," Corey persisted. "Or really, what it's *not* about. There's no mention of peace or hope or happiness. . . ."

"Oh please, Corey Man, shut the eff up, will you?" Lee said. "The song is about a battle—we fought for our freedom, for Christ's sakes. And the flag was still there!"

"Maybe Vonnegut was right," Jude said.

"Yeah, he's right," Corey agreed. "Counterculture, that's what I'm all about—whatever's out there, I'm against it!" Typical Corey. He had the rule-hating gene in his double helix.

"Yeah, but what are you *for*?" Lee asked.

"You know what I'm for?" Corey said. "I'm for . . . 'Oh, say, can you see . . .' that McDonald's up ahead? I'm for pulling into the drive-through. I'm starverated."

When they reached their haunted destination at 112 Ocean Avenue in the town of Amityville, Lee killed the lights and coasted curbside. The boys stared out the windows at the old, silent house. It was three stories high with seven windows facing the street, a few tall trees and a low, neatly manicured hedge set off a few feet from the front of the house. At a casual glance, it looked about as scary as a cucumber sandwich.

They had all been there before, even though the drive to Amityville was more than half an hour. There was something magnetic about the place. The house was famous for its ghostly legends, and the second-rate Hollywood movie that was based on all the weird stuff that happened after the DeFeo murders back in 1974, scaring the living daylights out of the next family that moved in until, one night, they fled the house and never returned. No one would ever know what really happened.

Lee turned around in his seat to once again retell the tale, his voice hushed and mysterious, drawing out the words to build suspense. "So after the murders, the Lutz family moved in," Lee began.

The boys had all heard it before, about as much as *Green Eggs and Ham*, but no one tried to shut Lee up. After all, it was his car and they were a long way from home.

"I guess they got a bargain price," Jude opined.

"Yeah, but after they moved in, all this sick shit started happening," Lee said. "Like, swarms of flies were everywhere, even in the winter. The father of the family used to wake up in a cold sweat every night at three fifteen—the exact same time of the murders. Green slime oozed from the walls. And one night they saw a demon's face in the flames of the fireplace."

"I'm calling bullshit," Canino said. "It was a hoax."

"Cheesy movie though," Jude said appreciatively.

"Hold that thought," Corey said. "I've got to take a leak." He climbed out of the car, forfeiting shotgun, and wandered off into some nearby bushes.

A minute later Corey scrambled into the backseat, laughing and gasping and still zipping up his jeans. "Go, go, go!" he shouted.

"What the hell?" Lee asked.

A fist pounded against the side window. It was a white-haired geezer who appeared like a vengeful ghost out of nowhere, sputtering and ranting at the boys, telling them to go away, they had no business here, *blah blah blah*. He was pretty excited for a grandpa. Stallion gave him the finger, and Lee hit the gas—four guys racing in the streets, a little buzzed and laughing, speeding into the heart of Saturday night and the start of Jude Fox's sixteenth summer on the planet.

TWELVE

Operation Becka swung into full effect. With Corey acting as Jude's spiritual adviser—"Go for it, Jude dude," was the sum of Corey's advice—Jude spent many hours deep in thought, meditating on Her Beckaness. At work Jude took every opportunity to make small talk, joke around, and take breaks with Becka. He even went so far as burning CDs for her, a lovesick act if ever there was one. He painstakingly selected each song for maximum meaning and full effect. The music would reveal to her his secret soul, his beating heart, his unspoken depths and innate goodness. They were, in other words, a bunch of really sad songs, one after another. All strummed in a minor key. Jude pushed the CDs into Becka's long thin fingers and jabbered about these really great tunes she absolutely had to hear.

And Becka, for her part, seemed to enjoy Jude's fumbling attention. She listened to the music, commented favorably on some of it, and threw pieces of stale pretzels at the seagulls. They often chatted during lunch breaks in the shade of a breezeway, a concrete passageway that connected the main concession building to the women's bathrooms and shower facilities. It was actually nicer than that sounds. Things with Becka usually were.

"What about your family?" she asked. "Do you have any brothers or sisters?"

"No, just me," Jude said. But that wasn't exactly true. So he clarified, told how he used to have a little sister, Lily, but she died, like, six years ago.

"I'm so sorry," Becka said. She reached out, put an open hand on his upper arm.

"Yeah, no, it's fine," Jude said. "I mean, it totally sucked, and I guess it still does sometimes, but you kind of get used to it." He looked away, uncomfortable and embarrassed, not used to it at all. He didn't want to talk about it, had already said too much.

"How did she—?"

Jude turned to her, eyes dull and brown. "I can't talk about it, Beck," he apologized. "Not now."

Becka nodded and didn't try to make it better. She just sat with him, silent, together. He loved that Becka didn't try to smooth it over with idle nothings, all the empty words like Band-Aids he'd heard over the years, how sad it was and how it must have been so hard for him and how terribly unfair everything was. People like his neighbor Mrs. Buchman, who prodded and poked and made sympathetic noises when all he ever wanted was to be left alone.

Jude was grateful that Becka didn't probe for facts.

"Hey, you know what?" Becka said. "I heard we're getting a new closing manager—that guy Roberto told us about."

"Kenny 'Half-Baked' Mays, the man, the myth, the legend," Jude said, grateful for the change of subject. "I'll believe it when I see it."

"Roberto says he's the coolest boss ever."

"Yeah, like Ernie from Sesame Street," Jude said.

"Ernie? What?" Becka asked, her eyes like bright beams, smiling.

"I guess this guy, Kenny Mays, is supposedly the biggest partier on the planet. They call him Half-Baked."

Becka laughed, "Half-Baked Mays—like the potato chips. Who comes up with this stuff? I don't know, it doesn't sound right. How does the world's biggest partier become a manager?"

Jude shrugged—no idea.

Becka seemed to chew on that for a while, ever the queen of speculation. Her face immediately brightened. "I just remembered. Did you see that notice about the softball game on the bulletin board? It's coming up."

Jude raised both hands. "Don't tell me, you're like a ninja when it comes to softball."

Becka blew on her fingernails, brushed them on her shirt. "Seriously? I've got mad skills. Are you going to come? It'll be fun. We totally need you—we can't lose to Field Six."

"No, that would be humiliating," Jude commented. "If you can give me a ride home, I'll play."

"Great!" Becka answered. And her smile was so genuine, her happiness so pure, it was all Jude could do to keep himself from leaning in and kissing her on the lips. He wanted to, but something stopped him. Not yet, not here, but they were close. On some unspoken level, Becka hadn't given him permission yet.

Uncertainty crept into Jude's thoughts.

Maybe she never would. Maybe they were falling head over heels into a mineshaft of disappointment called Let's Just Be Friends.

Ugh, anything but the F-word.

THIRTEEN

The cards came like clockwork around the date of Lily's birthday, June 28, though fewer arrived as the years passed. Jude's mother displayed the condolences and prayer cards on the refrigerator, then mercifully packed them away shortly after. Jude hated those cards, hated the way everyone knew about his "family tragedy"—poor Jude, that poor family. As if anyone knew how he felt, as if they had a damn clue.

His neighbor, Mrs. Buchman, was the worst, with that bittersweet smile, the way she always asked, "How are you, Jude? Everything okay?" She watched him with those eyes of hers, a gaze that looked upon him with such tenderness and pity that it burned his skin and made Jude turn away.

Lily had been playmates with the Buchman girls, forever bouncing on their trampoline, doing what little girls do. Drawing pictures, practicing cartwheels, chasing after cats. Lily used to say that Zoe Buchman was her best friend in the whole big world. Jude still saw Zoe out on the block. Ten years old now and skinny as a pole. They never talked, never said a word, just warily watched each other out of the corner of their eyes, thinking whatever it was they thought. Jude the older boy who cast a sad shadow, Zoe the gangly girl who once played inside his house, munching on fresh-baked cookies: strangers now.

Each year, on the anniversary of Lily's birthday, Mrs. Buchman left a basket of flowers on the front stoop. Pale yellow lilies of the valley, of course, always with a short, handwritten note attached. This year was no different. Jude almost tripped on them on his way out the door to Corey's. "Jesus Christ!" he muttered, and angrily kicked at the flowers. The basket crashed against the front door, the delicate petals in disarray, scattered on the ground.

His mother must have heard the noise, for she came to the door. They stared at each other through the window, Jude standing there, trembling with a rage he couldn't name; his mother's lips set in a frown, her eyes turned down to look at the mess of flowers on ground. *Click.* She started to push open the door, but Jude pressed his hand against it. "Don't," he said. "Please, Mom. I've got it."

He bent to his knees and one by one assembled the fallen flowers, painstakingly arranged them back in the basket. He picked up the card. It was plain and blue and read, *"Our thoughts are with you on this difficult day."*

Jude didn't have to say anything. Not to Corey. Because Corey knew. One look at Jude and he knew. Corey had that gift. And he said exactly the right thing: "Let's go whack some frakkin' golf balls." So they grabbed Corey's clubs and headed out together on foot, Corey talking nonstop while Jude's thundering heart slowly returned to normal and he could breathe again.

"So when am I going to meet this Becka babe?" Corey asked.

"I don't know if she's ready for you," Jude said.

Corey nodded thoughtfully. "All my manly manliness might be too much, huh? I can see that. Seriously, Jude—you've got to step up. How long are you going to like this girl without making a move?"

Jude didn't answer. He grabbed a golf ball from the bucket and set it on the tee. The two friends stood in an empty soccer field behind a nearby elementary school, a perfect spot for banging around golf balls. Nobody to bean in the head, no grandmas sprawled on the ground, blood gushing from their noses.

"You should invite her out with us sometime," Corey suggested. "We could double-date, catch a movie or something."

"'Double-date'?" Jude stepped away from the tee. Corey did not currently have a girlfriend, though different girls always seemed to set their sights on him. "What are you going to do? Go out and buy an inflatable doll?"

"Oh, big laugh," Corey replied. "Come on, dude. This Becka hotness must have a friend for me. See what you can do."

Jude shanked the ball to the right, tossed his driver to the ground. "I so suck at this sport," he complained.

"You're collapsing your right side," Corey pointed out. "You can't attack the ball like a Viking with a battle axe. It's got to be one smooth motion. Watch and learn, my friend." Corey set up a new ball on the tee and drove a long, arcing shot into the center distance.

Jude wasn't interested. "Whatever we do, let's not take 'em golfing." Even so, he was warming to the idea. Maybe it would work, take the pressure off, keep it loose. "I wouldn't call it a *date*, though, you know? It would be just hanging out."

"With benefits," Corey said.

Jude rolled his eyes. "I'm not sure about a movie, either. You can't talk to each other in a crowded theater. If you do, people throw Milk Duds at your head." This time Jude hit a beautiful ball, high and far. Corey, now seated cross-legged on the grass, whistled in appreciation.

"Three words, Jude."

"Yeah, and? What are they?"

"Make-out session."

"Oh, please," Jude said. "You'll be lucky if I can find a date for you."

"How about bowling?" Corey suggested. "We could do the

Rock 'n' Bowl at Alley Cat Lanes on Friday night. I heard they canned the deejay because he became obsessed with death metal. It was 'kill, hate, vomit, kill' song after song. It threw off everybody's game. Nothing but gutter balls and mayhem. Now they're hiring real bands."

"I don't know about bowling," Jude said.

"Dude, it's not about the score," Corey argued. "Nobody cares about that. It's all about the shoes. I'm dead sexy in a pair of two-toned, cream-colored bowling shoes," he joked, giving a halfway decent impression of Austin Powers.

Jude slid his club into the golf bag. "Let's pick 'em up," he said, ignoring his friend.

"Okay, boss," Corey joked. "Your balls are there, and over there, and way over there," he said, pointing at scattered spots on the empty field. He grinned at Jude. "So are you going to ask her or not?"

"Maybe." Jude got an idea. "How would you feel if your date's name was Roberto?"

"Roberto?"

"He's my friend from work."

"Oh," Corey said. "Well, that kind of throws a wrench into the make-out session. Can he bowl?"

"Doubtful," Jude grinned.

Corey slid a club into the golf bag, hoisted it on his shoulder. "I like seeing you like this. You've changed."

"Oh?"

"Yeah, you're happy," Corey said.

Jude made a face. "What are you talking about? I've been happy."

"Okay, whatever. I don't know," Corey said, considering Jude. "Lighter maybe. Something's different. I think this girl's good for you. But one thing hasn't changed. You still suck at golf."

FOURTEEN

It was true. Jude was happy. He sat in the back of the car, pleased to see that he'd managed to bring together two friends from different worlds, Corey and Roberto.

Roberto was wearing a brown *Big Lebowski* bowling shirt; it read, THE DUDE MINDS, MAN. So tacky it rocked the house. He had borrowed the family car, a red Taurus, and Corey was stationed in the shotgun seat. It was a kick for Jude to sit back and watch those two together—a satisfying feeling.

It was Friday night, and the boys were headed to the Rock 'n' Bowl out on Sunrise Highway. The double-date idea didn't work out with Becka. She had called in sick for work that morning. Jude texted her, and they bounced a couple of messages back and forth. Becka said she was under the weather and taking it slow for the weekend. So Jude never asked her, exactly. He invited Roberto instead. A mini brodown, second degree.

"Could we make a short detour, Berto?" Jude asked.

Corey turned around, one eyebrow arched, suspicious. "Where to?"

"I'm going over to Becka's house soon; we're supposed to jam together. I was thinking—I kind of wanted to scope out where she lives," Jude said, and felt instantly naked for saying so, fully revealed for the lovesick sap he'd truly become.

"So you're like a stalker now?" Roberto asked, eyes twinkling in the rearview mirror.

Corey laughed, a loud bark, and Roberto jiggled his head, body shaking.

"Our boy's got it bad," Corey confided to Roberto. "Jude is besotted."

"Besotted?" Jude echoed. "What the hell?"

"Really, Jude, come on," Corey said, enjoying himself. "Drive by her house? What do you want to do after that? Go to Build-A-Bear?"

"Wait a minute," Roberto interrupted. "You're going to jam with her, but you've never even heard her play guitar?"

Jude nodded. "Yeah. I bet she's good, though."

"Good? Who gives a crap?" Corey said. "You could strap a guitar around, I don't know, the mummified corpse of Mother Theresa, and she'd be sexy as hell. It's the ultimate turn-on."

Roberto nodded, grinning. "He's right, Jude. That's the power of rock and roll. Any girl is ten times hotter if she plugs into an amp."

"That's what I'm talking about," Corey said; he fist-bumped Roberto.

Roberto glanced back at Jude. "Man, you're so whipped," he said. "*Oh, Becka, sweetheart, I love your luminous eyes*," Roberto purred in a high-pitched falsetto. "*They are like limpid pools of* . . . I don't know what the frak."

" 'Frak'?!" Corey repeated, laughing. "You're a *Battlestar Galactica* fan?"

"Oh, yeah, big-time," Roberto said. "I have the complete series on DVD. Best sci-fi show ever. I could power disk that shit all night long."

"Adama's the man," Corey said.

"Don't even get me started on Kara Thrace," Roberto replied.

"I'm more into Number Six," Corey admitted.

"Ohhhh, she's a bad, bad Cylon," Roberto joked.

Corey turned in his seat, grinned at Jude. "Nice shirt, by the way," he said, noting Jude's pastel polo.

"Yeah, does it come in guy colors?" Berto cracked.

Jude laughed along with his friends, told them it was only a matter of time before they had a show together on Bravo. Besides, they were kind of right. Lately he couldn't think of much else besides Becka. She kept creeping into his thoughts. At work he was attuned to her every movement; watched her at the cash register, knew exactly when she took breaks, and tried whenever possible to arrange quasi-accidental time together. Becka, for her part, sent signals the same way. There was something definitely going on between them. Some sort of dance. Where it was all headed . . . Jude didn't know.

Roberto blew off Jude's request to visit Becka's house and drove directly to the Alley Cat Lanes. "Don't be mad, Jude. We'll hide in her bushes another time," Roberto half apologized.

"Oh, yeah, we'll have all the handy stalker tools," Corey chimed in. "GPS tracker, night-vision goggles, whatever it takes to get you hooked up, my brother."

Jude felt there was something undeniably cheesy and yet thrilling about your basic Rock 'n' Bowl experience. It was like a bizarro blend of the coolest things you could imagine and the lamest things ever, like, um, *bowling* itself, all mixed together. The Alley Cat was packed with teenagers and college kids, most of the girls wearing complicated haircuts and expensive denim. Some guys did the cliché thing and wore vintage, two-toned bowling shirts with thick vertical stripes, others saw it as an opportunity to impress the girls with their bulging biceps, a trick that required wearing T-shirts that were two sizes too small. It was a wonder they could swing their arms.

Roberto poked Jude, whistled softly, said that watching the redhead in lane six bend over to pick up a ball was alone worth the price of admission. Four center lanes were reserved for the band, a five-piece outfit that was actually not too bad. Very jam bandy, they were covering a Dave Matthews tune when the guys walked in, and not without skill. It sounded good, featured a propulsive groove, but at the same time, you didn't have to pay attention to the band, either. The right sounds for Rock 'n' Bowl. The place was all dark corners and cheap laser lights, punctuated by the clatter of crashing pins. It had been a while since Jude had been to the Alley Cat, and he was happy to be back, hearing the pins rumble like thunder. Jude was sure that half the crowd was buzzed on something, tripping the light fantastic. With that many guys and girls jumbled in one place, rock music blaring, strobes flashing, it felt like what school might have been like without the teachers and hall monitors.

Corey, Roberto, and Jude settled into their assigned lane to the far left of the cavernous alley. Jude typed in the names, which were displayed on an overhead screen, while Roberto read aloud from a paper place mat he'd picked up off the floor. "Did you know that bowling is the number-one participation sport in America?" he enthused. "More than seventy million people bowl annually!"

"These lights are very *Dark Side of the Moon*," Corey observed, only half listening.

"I'm getting a pitcher of Coke," Roberto announced. "Anyone need anything?"

"Curly fries," Jude said.

"I'll take the redhead in lane six," Corey ordered. "To go!"

When Roberto returned, he poured a plastic glass for Jude. "Here," he said.

Jude took a sip, then instantly reared back to look into the cup. "What the hell?"

"Captain Morgan sails again," Roberto said. "*Arrrr*, yo-ho-ho, me mateys. I smuggled in a bottle of rum!"

"I don't know," Jude demurred. "You're driving, Roberto."

"Trust me, Lumbus," Roberto said. "I'll take it easy, just a drink or two. I'm not going to get all freak-tarded."

Corey grabbed his glass and tapped it against Roberto's. "Here's to grog and wenches and designated drivers," he said, and drank deeply.

The games got progressively sloppier as they goofed their way through the night. They rolled and drank, bowled and slurped, with Roberto keeping their glasses full. At first they watched the scoreboard, kept a brisk pace, and pretended to care. But after a while, Roberto dropped out entirely, claiming boredom; he preferred to provide color commentary from the back table. True to his word, Roberto sipped slowly on his rum and Coke, but it made him more talkative than ever. After a poor shot from Jude that left pins at each end, Roberto announced, "Hey, split happens."

And when Corey missed an easy spare, Roberto lamented, "Corey, you're being very undude right now."

Corey shrugged, held up his hands in a gesture of indifference.

"Jude, dude. Look down there to the right," Roberto suddenly instructed. "Way down on the far side of the band. Is that Becka?"

Jude didn't see her at first. The place was dark. But Roberto was right. The band was getting ready to take a break. Becka stood at the top of the lane, amid a small throng of fans. She looked great and clapped enthusiastically.

Becka? What is she doing here?

"Which one's her?" Corey was eager to know. "I'm dying to get a look at Jude's future wife."

Jude picked up a ball, stood a little unsteadily, got set to roll another. His brain didn't seem to be fully functioning, like a slow computer that couldn't download the information fast enough.

"What the frak?" Roberto said. "Stop bowling, Jude! Go say hi."

"Yeah, bring her back here," Corey urged. "I want to meet this girl."

Jude felt lit and loose and Becka was actually here, now. It was like the hand of fate. His friends were right. He'd go find her, say hello. *Why not?* Jude looked across the lanes. He'd lost sight of her. Becka was somewhere between the strobe lights and shadows.

"She's going to *love* you in those shoes," Corey said. "Believe me, they are total babe magnets. This is the night."

Jude smiled, flung the ball carelessly down the lane, didn't look back. "Back in a flew—I mean, *a few*," he said, a little slurry.

The band had stopped, so more people seemed to mill around the carpeted area behind the lanes. Jude walked slowly, craning his neck, looking for Becka. Where was she? When he saw her, Jude stopped cold. She was seated with a group of older-looking guys. Well, not seated *with*. Seated *on*.

She was sitting on some long-haired guy's lap.

Jude watched from fifty feet away as Becka fed the boy a french fry. She laughed, playful, bare-shouldered, gorgeous. Becka had a hand around the boy's shoulder. Jude knew she had a couple of older brothers. But he could imagine Roberto's voice in his ear: *"Dude, I don't think that's her brother."*

No, this guy was the drummer in the band. *The drummer!* Probably drove a freaking love van with cheap carpet in the back. A night's worth of rum and coke mainlined to Jude's brain, fogging his thoughts. He spun, turned, staggered as if punched, more buzzed than he realized, and made his way back to Corey and Roberto.

"We gotta go, we gotta go right now," Jude announced.

"Sit down, man," Roberto said. "Pull up a chair. I can't drive for at least another hour."

"I don't care," Jude said. "We'll walk, whatever. I'm leaving *now*." Jude bolted, had to get out of there, the spinning lights, the crowds. He fled in search of fresh air.

Corey and Roberto exchanged glances, followed Jude out the side door.

"You all right?" It was Corey in Jude's ear, holding him by the upper arm. "What happened?"

"She's playing Santa with the drummer—the freaking drummer!" Jude sputtered.

They eventually got the story out of him, not that it was anything new: Boy meets girl, girl rips heart out of boy's chest, feasts on his entrails. Welcome to the zombie apocalypse. Same old, same old. Corey wrapped an arm around Jude's shoulders, steadied him. "The high school isn't far from here. We can hang by the bleachers, howl at the moon. You'll be okay." He turned to Roberto. "Can you go back inside and smuggle out a pitcher of Coke?"

"Aye-aye, me bucko," Roberto grinned.

Three messy hours later, with great concentrated effort, Jude slid the key into his front door. It was late, past midnight. The house was dark. He felt tired, beat. Grabbed the banister by the stairs and groaned. Something caught his eye. Jude paused, stopped. "Mom, I didn't see you there."

She was in her bathrobe, sitting in the dark, waiting for her boy to come home.

"I couldn't sleep," she said. "Have you been drinking?"

Jude considered the question, brain misfiring. "It's okay, Mom," Jude said. "I'm home now. I'm going to bed. You should too."

He looked at her from across the room. Her hair was beginning to turn white, her eyes were pink and small. She seemed frail, fragile. She had never been the same. Ever since Lily passed, his mother was present and absent at once. Here and not here.

Jude took a few steps up the stairs, almost losing his balance. He sat down on the fifth step, elbows on his knees, head in his hands.

His mother rose and took a tentative step toward him. "Are you going to be all right? Jude? Can I help you?"

He shook his head, "No, no. It's just . . . tonight sucked." He looked up, steadied his gaze, watched his mother stare at him. Her arms dangled uselessly at her sides, like a marionette with severed strings.

She didn't move, frozen in place; didn't speak, unable to find the words.

"Good night, Mom," Jude finally said, slowly rising. "Love you."

She nodded imperceptibly in the dark, a movement he did not catch, and otherwise made no reply.

Heart clouded in confusion, Jude climbed the stairs and fell—dreamlessly, noiselessly, thoughtlessly—into bed.

FIFTEEN

Jude hit the snooze button three times before rising. He felt sour, his mouth stale and parched, his teeth wearing sweaters after a night of too much rum and coke and heartache. The house was silent. Jude shambled into the bathroom for a long, reviving shower. It helped. Failing to find a fresh work shirt, Jude fished the cleanest dirty shirt from the hamper. Sniffed it, frowned: *pretty ripe.* The shirt matched his mood. Mad at the world.

In the kitchen, Jude gulped a tall glass of orange juice. A note on the counter informed him that his father had gone out for a long, slow run. His father ran to get away from it all, yet despite all the hours logged and miles slogged, he always returned to the same place; the road never rose to lift him to some new, shimmering elsewhere.

Jude considered himself a different kind of runner entirely. First of all, his father *jogged*; Jude *ran.* Big diff. His father was one of those old guys who stopped after his run, winded and panting, two fingers on his neck, counting the beats of his pulse while he stared at the watch on his wrist. Goofy shit, if you asked Jude. A lot of times, Jude headed out in just a pair of shorts. No shirt, no shoes, a barefoot runner in the burbs. Nobody could say nothing, because Jude was faster than them all.

His mother was a notorious late riser; Jude rarely saw her before he left for work. He knew he should eat, so cracked three eggs into a bowl, scrambled them with a fork, and added a splash of milk while a slab of butter sizzled in the skillet. Jude tossed torn pieces of ham into a second, smaller pan. He had grown into a capable cook, and ham and cheese omelets were his specialty. His mother wasn't big on sit-down meals these days—or had the days becomes years?—so Jude was used to fending for himself. She used to have a job, selling medical supplies, but after Lily passed, things changed. She eventually got laid off for missing too many days and . . .

After Lily passed.

That phrase again.

Those three words like a sword that severed his life in two.

It was how everyone talked. Empty words in hushed, polite tones. *After Lily passed.*

Passed? *Past?* And what of the present? It was defined by absence, what was no longer there. The empty mirror after someone walks away.

Lily was dead and that was that, no other way to skin the cat, yet she came to his mind every day. A visitor, a neighbor ringing the bell. Here to borrow a cup of sugar? Or with some other intent? Why ask why. Sometimes he called for her, conjured up images like a sorcerer. Lily at play, her lithe body wriggling inside a hula-hoop, the family cheering, "Go, girl, go!" The two of them drawing shoulder to shoulder on the hardwood floor. At Lily's urging, Jude copied comics from the newspaper and she colored them in. He laughed at her crazy color schemes. The grass blue, the sun green, the sky a cockamamy blaze of orange and pink. Lily never saw anything wrong with it, and neither did Jude.

Most days he didn't try to remember. But Lily would come to him unbidden, a spectral figure, a holographic image projected from the dreamworld ether. He would pass a playground and see her, like a vision, sitting idly on a swing as if waiting for a push. Or out on his own street, he'd see one of Lily's old playmates riding a bicycle—little Zoe Buchman, older now, still growing, still alive—and the memories would come flooding back, drowning his thoughts with images and phrases. He remembered those silly songs she used to sing—*"Baa, baa, black sheep, have you any pizza?"*—her smiles, and her laughter. He remembered how his father had packed her things in boxes and stored them in the attic. But for the most part, Lily's room remained unchanged, untouched by time: His mother had insisted on that. Jude dared not enter—after ever after—but could still picture it: that enormous stuffed bear in the corner, the posters of ballerinas on pink walls.

Gone, and yet she was everywhere.

He missed her so much.

They had turned her room into a kind of shrine, a mausoleum filled with her playthings. It was weird and upsetting, Jude thought. His mother called it the guest room, but who was she kidding? Nobody came. It was the Lily Museum, an internment room for her spirit. Jude looked at it once and never returned, nor did his father, but sometimes he'd catch his mother in there, sitting quietly in a chair, the door open, hands folded in her lap, as if waiting for a bus or something else to take her away.

His cell vibrated. Becka—again. She had tried him twice last night, and twice Jude ignored the messages before finally powering off altogether. He didn't have the heart for it. Not yet. Had she seen him at the bowling alley? Snatched a glimpse as he stood there, watching her? Or as he turned, walking away? Did she merely want to give him a ride to work?

Jude had briefly considered running—it would be good to sweat out the toxins, clear his head—but he knew there was no life in his legs this morning.

He took the bus.

Becka was already at work, seated behind a register. Jude managed to stay busy, avoid eye contact. Jessup looked haggard, slumped in a chair at his desk, puffy around the eyes. Allergies or something worse. "You look like hell," Jude said, not unsympathetically.

Jessup nodded, said he felt worse than that, told Jude in a hoarse voice to go clean up the picnic area. Jude grabbed a soapy washrag, bucket, and broom to wander among the yellow tables, searching the ground for fallen fries, used napkins, fluttering hot dog wrappers, assorted windswept litter. Most people didn't bother clearing their tables after eating, figuring that somebody else would clean up after them. They figured right about that—somebody would, some sucker with a fierce hangover named Jude Fox.

He felt confused and angry, a bitter taste on the back of his tongue. Out of old habit, Jude tried to push his thoughts aside, focus on the bright morning sunshine, but it was useless. The same unhappy feelings yammered at his brain. Corey had tried to console Jude last night, hauling out that stale line about how there were plenty more fish in the sea. "Don't obsess, Jude," Corey advised. "She's one girl. There are lots more babes out there. Look around. It's a beautiful planet."

Jude knew Corey didn't believe a word of it. Neither of them looked at girls that way. Becka wasn't another fish in the sea, some flat-bellied flounder in the deep blue water. Becka was different, special. They had a connection, Jude knew it. And this one hurt.

He checked the garbage cans, using cardboard trays to push down the contents, hoping he wouldn't find one that had to be emptied. But it was part of the job, the grunt work, and when necessary, he pulled up the bulging, soggy plastic liners, tied them off, and inserted a new liner into each grimy, foul-smelling can. He half dragged, half carried the torn, dripping, disgusting bags over to the Dumpster around back. Good times.

Roberto found Jude by the Dumpster. "He's coming!" Roberto exclaimed. "Jessup is going home sick. They're shifting him over to West End Two."

Jude's brain was fogged. He didn't understand.

"Kenny Mays," Roberto said. "He's filling in for Denzel."

"Have you got a man crush on this guy?" Jude asked. "I'm starting to wonder about you, Roberto—not that there's anything wrong with that."

"Shut up, Lumbus," Roberto replied. "You'll see." Then he returned to his post behind the counter, practically skipping with excitement. Jude sighed. He felt like crawling into the Dumpster for a nap.

The new manager, Kenny Mays, arrived when Jude was working the grill. Kenny was smallish with a large beak, a college boy with wavy hair that grew below his ears. Jude watched through sidelong glances as Kenny moved through the crew, introducing himself, learning names. There didn't seem anything particularly wonderful about him, but at the same time, he seemed real. Unpretentious. Kenny slipped a hot pretzel from the warmer and took a bite. He turned to Jude. "Did you make this?"

Jude shook his head, pointed to Emilio.

"Emilio, right?" Kenny asked. "When did you make the pretzels?"

Emilio shrugged. "I don't know, when I first came in, a couple of hours ago."

"Here, take a bite." Kenny ripped off a length of pretzel and handed it to Emilio, who chewed it thoughtfully.

"Are you proud of that pretzel?" Kenny asked.

Emilio glanced at Jude, shifted his eyes back to the new manager, wondering if he was getting punked or some other kind of joke. "It's a pretzel." He shrugged.

"No offense," Kenny said, "but it tastes like an old shoe that's been peed on by a dog."

Emilio stopped chewing, swallowed.

"Pull all those out, throw 'em away," Kenny said. "You can't leave pretzels hanging in that warmer for too long; they turn to cardboard." He instructed Emilio to make another batch, not so much salt this time. Less brown, more golden.

As the day dragged on, Kenny remained a ball of energy. Bouncing from one place to the other, joking with the crew, grabbing two strong guys and getting them to rearrange the kegs in the walk-in refrigerator, and on and on. He worked hard and made everyone else work hard too. That's when Jude realized that it was like a guitar, all about *tone*. Not what you said, but *how* you said it. The words were just words, standard grammatical units, *floating on sound*. The weird thing was, Jude now understood, the sound meant more than the words themselves. You could say "close the door" eight hundred different ways. But Kenny could tell you to clean out the toilets in such a way that you'd race into the bathrooms, eager to swab away. He had a gift for making every task sound good.

In the late afternoon, with things slowing down, Kenny pulled Jude aside. "Hey, Jude, hey, Jude, hey, Judy, Judy, Jud-EEE!" he sang, as countless others had done before him. "You know this crew better than I do. Who do I send home, and who do I keep for the big rodeo?"

Jude arched his eyebrows. "A rodeo? Like a yee-ha kind of thing?"

"Closing this place, breaking it down, cleaning it up. I need real workers—no slackers," Kenny said.

"How many?" Jude asked.

"Four guys and two cashiers."

Jude pointed out a few likely crew members, Ivan, Roberto, and DaJon, the mustached twenty-one-year-old with a silky manner who was old enough to pour beer. DaJon was a good guy. Jude looked across the floor to the three cashiers who remained: Daphne, Becka, and the unlovely lump Margorie Watson, aka Sourpuss. "Maybe Daphne and Margorie?" he suggested.

Kenny laughed, took it like a joke. "Right, large Marge in charge. She looks like fun." He picked Becka instead.

Jude had steered clear of Becka all day, even worked through his break to avoid her. He resisted a dozen urges to confront her about last night. If Becka noticed, she didn't push things, just did her job and kept a distance.

Kenny went around, thanking guys, sending them home, until his handpicked skeleton crew remained. Once the last customers were served, Kenny locked the door and yelled, "All right, let's knock this out and get out of Dodge."

Kenny energized the entire crew. They worked like whirling dervishes for the next twenty minutes—scraping the grill, emptying the grease trays, cleaning up behind the counter, washing the windows, sweeping and mopping the floors. Kenny brought up a little portable Bose system, plugged in his iPod, and the walls shook with a crazy mix of hard-core rap and metal. By the end, the place was spotless. Unlike Denzel, who left every night with clean fingernails, Kenny labored right along with everyone else, really putting his back into it. Jude noticed Roberto cleaning out a large, plastic, gallon-size mustard jar. "What are you doing, Berto?" Jude asked.

Roberto grinned. "Kenny's idea. Our reward for a job well done."

While the crew punched out, Roberto filled two mustard jars with beer from the tap. DaJon stood watch by the back door.

"Don't let anybody see you guys," Kenny said. "Throw a towel or something over it."

"You going to hang with us, Kenny?" Roberto asked.

Kenny shook his head. "People to do, things to meet. Just be sure to get away from the building. Go to the far end of the parking lot—over by the dunes. If you get caught, I don't know anything about it."

Off they went, the jolly crew, smuggling mustard jars of

pale ale into the sand dunes. It gave them a feeling of giddiness, a happy euphoria: beer, because they earned it. A bunch of working stiffs on their way to the neighborhood dive. Not enough beer to get hammered or anything, or even fail a Breathalyzer test, just enough to take the edge off a long day.

The only ones left were Jude, Roberto, DaJon, Ivan, Daphne, and Becka. Roberto opined that no way in hell he was walking across that hot parking lot—"I'd rather play hopscotch on the surface of the sun"—so he rolled over in his mother's wheels with DaJon and Ivan.

Becka got her car too and offered Jude and Daphne a ride. "No, I'm good," Jude said. "I'll walk. You guys go." Becka gave him a quizzical look, like, *Are you for real?* So he relented and climbed into the backseat. In the hot car, Jude felt tense and uncomfortable. Fortunately, Daphne seemed oblivious to the tension and chattered about her volunteer work at some pet-rescue center. "I'm not kidding," she said. "After the old lady died, we discovered there were more than seventy-five cats living in her house."

"Oh, my God," Becka gasped.

"You should have seen it, Beck. They were sick and undernourished; my heart was breaking the whole time. It was horrible and disgusting."

"Didn't anyone notice?" Jude asked.

"That's what I said," Daphne replied, shifting in her seat to look back at Jude. "It was just this old, lonely woman who lived by herself—"

"With, like, a million cats," Jude said.

"It makes me sad," Becka commented. "That poor lady."

"Those poor *cats*," Daphne corrected.

They parked and gathered in a loose circle in a depression amid the dunes, pulling off shoes and socks, feeling the scrunch of warm sand between their toes. Roberto complained about seagulls, "rats with wings," he called them.

Jude glanced at Daphne to see if she'd react. She probably liked rats. But the thin girl with large eyes had her head tilted toward Becka, deep in some kind of whispered conference.

DaJon took a swig from the mustard jar, wiped his mouth with the back of his arm. "They say that about pigeons. Rats with wings."

"Sure, if you live in the city, it's pigeons," Berto conceded. "Out here, it's seagulls. People think they are so beautiful soaring in the wind, but those people should come over with me to the Dumpster sometime. I'll show 'em what seagulls are all about." He took a shallow sip of beer, shivered, and said, "Nasty beasts."

Roberto had a way of claiming the spotlight without overdoing it. He told hilarious stories about his Cuban grandmother Mam-Maw, and kept the conversation rolling. Roberto was in full glory, mid-story, saying, "At first I was like, '*What*?' then I was like, '*WHAT*?!' " when Jude's cell vibrated.

Why r u so weird today?

Jude read the text and glanced at its sender, sitting across from him. Becka looked back at him, worry in her eyes.

She rose and stretched. "I'm walking down to the water for a minute. Come with me, Jude."

Phrased that way, Jude didn't have much choice. Roberto cast a hairy eyeball at Jude and offered a slight, almost imperceptible shrug. "Good luck with that," he seemed to say.

SIXTEEN

Jude and Becka walked in silence to the water's edge. Becka put a stick of gum in her mouth. Jude thought of all the gum he scraped from the table and, *screw it*, asked for a piece anyway.

"Open a pack of gum and suddenly everybody's your friend," Becka joked.

Jude smiled—he couldn't help himself—and took the gum from her hand. The late-afternoon surf was nearly perfect, the waves rolling in rhythmic succession before breaking and thundering to the sand, like white horses galloping to the shore. "Broken waves," Jude murmured. He listened to the drone of the sea's white noise, imagined it as a musical soundscape, a song, and felt the dry sting of salt air on his skin.

Becka rolled her pants to the knees and waded a few feet into the warm, low surf. "You ever go skinny-dipping in the ocean?" she asked. "It's religious."

Jude didn't comment. The girl had no clue. He saw that

the beach had slowly emptied out, only stragglers remained, families squeezing out the last minutes of pleasure before getting into their cars, a few joggers in both directions, a lone fisherman casting a line into the ocean, back bent and eternally hopeful.

"We should head back," Jude said.

"They'll wait."

"Yeah, but—"

"I saw you," Becka said. "At the bowling alley last night."

Jude picked up an oyster shell, rubbed his thumb across its ridges.

"I looked up and you were there," Becka continued. "Then you were gone."

Jude snapped the shell between his fingers. It was dry and brittle from too much exposure to the sun. He rolled his eyes, looked to the sky, watched clouds assemble. He felt an anger pulse through his body, rising up in his throat. "You know why," was all he could muster.

"I can explain, Jude."

"I don't care," he lied. He stepped closer to her in the water. "You should have told me, that's all. You lied to me, Beck. You said you were sick, you weren't going out. Is he your boyfriend?"

Becka shook her head no. She fidgeted with the strings of her hoodie. "I hate it when one string becomes longer than the other," she said, frowned, shrugged, stalling for time.

"I just thought that . . ." he stopped talking, couldn't find the end of the sentence. He wasn't used to talks like this, letting her inside. His instinct was to flee, just turn and head east along the shore, and run, run for miles.

Somehow she kept him there, water to his knees, this girl with tangled hair.

"Jude, I know you can't understand, but I really need to try to explain. It's important."

Jude crossed his arms, nodded. He'd listen.

"I've had this stupid crush on that guy—his name is Brian, by the way, if it matters to you—ever since I was in junior high," she said. Becka was talking quickly now, in a hurry to get the confession over, receive her penance. "He's friends with my brother, been coming to our house for years. And all this time, I've been, like, invisible, Matt's little sister."

Jude didn't want to hear the details. The ocean droned on, churning like a malevolent machine.

"Then last night—"

Jude interrupted her. "You don't have to explain anything to me. I'm just a friend, right?"

"I saw you," Becka said in a louder voice. She locked her gaze on his eyes, until they were the only two people in the world, just Jude and Becka. "And I felt like such a jerk."

A bubble of hope burbled up Jude's chest. He suppressed it and waited.

"I used to obsess over this guy," Becka said. "My big brother's friend. He was always there and he never saw me. Then last night, for the first time, he did. And it kind of threw me off balance. And the funny thing is, Jude, he's a total creep when it comes to girls. I knew it the moment I saw you walk away. I mean, I've always known it—Brian is like the biggest egomaniac on the planet, and we have nothing in common except for my brother."

"So you're saying it's over?" Jude looked away, afraid of the answer.

"I'm saying," she said, "that you're the one I like."

Jude watched a big wave roll in, building and gathering from behind Becka. He reached out his hands, said, "Hold on." The water hit her from behind, about shoulder high and with force, pushing her into his arms. She lurched forward, stumbling, and before he knew it, they were both knocked down in the water, twisting in the undertow.

"Are we okay?" Becka asked, struggling to her feet, clothes soaked through. There was urgency in her voice, almost panic. "I really want us to be okay."

Jude said, yeah, they were okay. But in his secret heart, full of shadows and unkempt corners, he honestly had no idea. She baffled him, and yet he ached for her even in his puzzlement.

"Let's get back to the others," he said.

Becka smiled and her face glowed, as if lit by candles. She was a natural beauty, no doubt about that. "We're already wet, might as well go swimming." Becka tugged at his hand, pulled him deeper into the ocean. And there she turned and waited, timing the surf before diving headfirst just as another perfect wave broke and shattered. Jude followed into the crash of roiling water, pounded by a hundred charging hooves, until he bobbed to the calm surface again, the sky still blue, the sunrays like diamonds glittering across the water, Becka beside him, eyes beaming, a searchlight on rocky shores.

SEVENTEEN

"What do you want to hear?" Jude asked. He sat cross-legged on a blanket in the park, holding an acoustic guitar. Becka reclined on her side, languid, liquid almost, and lazily replied, "Just play."

He wasn't nervous. With a guitar in his hands, Jude felt confident, at home. He went through some songs that he knew would impress her, sometimes fingerpicking, mostly knocking out easy riffs and asking her to "name that tune."

"You're a different person with a guitar," Becka observed.

"Different? How?" he asked.

"My guitar teacher Jess—he's crazy good, by the way, plays in the Centipedes—talks about something he calls a musical personality, which can be totally different from a person's ordinary personality."

"So somebody could be quiet in everyday life," Jude said, "but strap a guitar on him, and he turns into an extrovert." Jude mulled it over. "Sure, that makes sense to me."

They talked music for a while, swapped the names of favorite bands. For some reason, Jude found himself going overboard about his love for the Cure, in his words, "one of the most underrated bands ever."

Becka wasn't convinced. "I don't know, kind of old, aren't they?"

"Uh-oh," Jude said. "If you don't love the song 'Pictures of You,' I don't think we can be friends."

"Oh, well, it was nice while it lasted," Becka joked. "Do you write songs?"

"No," he lied. He had written quite a few, in fact, each one more fabulously bad than the last. The songs would stay buried in the vault.

"Really? I'm surprised. You seem so . . . *inside*."

"What do you mean?"

Becka paused, picking her words carefully as if they were shells in the sand. "It's like, with you, it's not all on the surface. There's something underneath."

Jude could live with that, *hidden depths*, secrets, and he didn't disagree.

"Sing something," Becka suggested.

Jude ran his fingers along the fretboard, pentatonic scales he'd played a million times, shook his head. "Um, no," he said. "I can't sing."

"Yeah, you can," Becka said. "Just open your mouth. Everybody can sing."

"Not me," Jude answered. He put down the guitar, reached

for some bread and cheese. It was Becka's idea—this picnic in the park—and she had brought everything to make it just so: a blanket, bread, cheese, fresh strawberries.

She took up the guitar, strumming hard, and sang in a high, clear voice, and it was Jude's turn to watch, to marvel. She was so natural about it, authentically herself, as confident as a flower opening its petals to the sun.

"My friend Corey wants to meet you," Jude said between songs.

"Oh, yeah?" Becka grinned. "Sounds like a big deal. Epic, almost. Is that like bringing me home to your parents? I get to meet Corey?"

"Yeah, it's exactly like that," Jude said, straight-faced. "I was thinking I could invite him to the softball game Wednesday night."

Becka nodded, strummed absentmindedly. "Can he hit?"

Jude shrugged. "Corey is one of those guys who can do anything, but he's more into pop culture than playing sports. Movies, books, music. He works at the bike store on Wantagh Avenue, near the train station. Supersmart guy." Jude didn't fully understand why, but he needed for Becka to know Corey, to like him. And, he guessed, for Corey to like her. It was probably dumb, but he wanted the dots to connect, like the stars of the Big Dipper. Jude, Becka, Corey, all friends. He'd seen a lot of guys get new girlfriends, and suddenly they were, like, gone. Vinnie did that a lot. He'd hook up with a girl and disappear for weeks, like a spy who'd gone deep cover. Jude didn't want it to be that way with Becka; he wanted her to fit into his world, and that world began with Corey, his best friend.

Becka shifted and lay on her back, resting her head in Jude's lap. Looking skyward, she observed, "It's a tie-dye sky."

Jude laughed. Only Becka could see the world that way. He admired how alive she was to things, the minor miracles of the everyday world.

She picked up a strawberry, brought it to her nose, and breathed in. It reminded Jude of one of the first days he saw her, that little nibble she took of the pretzel. "You eat like a rabbit, you know that?"

Becka poked out her two front teeth, twitched her nose. "I always smell my food," she said. "A habit, I guess. *A rabbit habit.* Do you think it's weird?"

"No, I like bunny rabbits," Jude said.

"Lie next to me," she told him. "Let your hands drop down to your sides."

Jude scooted down beside her, content under the tie-dye sky, all blues and purples and shifting clouds.

"I always think of the earth as a round ball, just spinning in space," Becka said. "Close your eyes. Can you feel it?"

Jude tried to imagine the great curve of the earth, like he was lounging across some giant exercise ball. It wasn't working so great, but he did like the feel of Becka's body next to his. They were in the middle of a grassy meadow, sparse with itinerant commuters, dog walkers, and Frisbee players, but they all dropped away, and Jude felt entirely at peace with this singular girl.

"It's a miracle we don't fly away," Becka said, her voice a whisper. "The earth spinning around and around—you'd think we'd just fall off."

"Gravity," Jude said.

"Science," Becka scoffed dismissively. "Don't think so much. Can't you feel it in your fingertips, the curve of the earth?"

Jude listened to the distant voices of a family carrying across the field, felt the lingering warmth of the near-evening air. He knew what Becka wanted him to say, so he said it. "Yes, I feel it—sort of."

He remembered something and told her a story. "When Lily, my sister, was little, she used to have all these stuffed animals, you know. We had this big ceiling fan in the living room. I was about five years older than her, so I used to climb up on this little step stool, and put all her stuffed animals on the blades of the fan."

"You were teasing her?" Becka asked.

"No, she loved it," Jude said. "Once it was all set up, I'd climb down and let her flick on the wall switch." He allowed himself a smile and soft laugh at the memory. "The blades would turn slowly at first, but one by one the animals would fly off. We'd make bets on which one would hang on the longest. Lily laughed so hard. She'd ask me to do it over and over again."

Becka sank into the grass, basking in the story's warm glow. "Nice," she said.

"Yeah, yeah, it was," Jude said. "I haven't thought of that in a long time. Funny I'm telling you this."

A quiet came over them, but not a silence that needed to be broken. It was not awkward or uncomfortable.

Finally, Becka spoke. "When things get too complicated," she confessed, "when I begin to take myself too seriously, I try to remember this feathery feeling. Like I could just float off the earth and fly away."

"Specks on a spinning globe," he said, thinking of it as *whirled*, not world, a revolving mystery, drifting like dust in a tie-dye sky, or animals hurled from the blades of a ceiling fan.

"We're tiny parts of this immense universe," Becka murmured. "Like flowers in a great garden."

Jude remembered that feeling when he was a little boy, turning round and round in his backyard, dizzy and falling to the ground. Drunk with wonder. He hadn't felt that way in a long, long time. Usually he felt more likely to sink to the earth's dark core than to levitate into the sky.

"Does it make you feel insignificant?" he asked.

"Not at all," Becka said, her voice soft, mellow. "I feel like I'm blessed, part of some unknowable mystery." They lay in silence together. "Are your eyes still closed?"

"Yes."

He sensed her movement, rising on an elbow. He felt her lips on his mouth, and they kissed.

"Thank you for forgiving me," she said.

Jude couldn't locate the name for this feeling, the string of a child's helium balloon slipping through his fingers, this sense of floating skyward, knew only a boy's confusion and thrill and desire, the heart's thrup and thrum. Kiss me again and again until all the stars crowd the sky like scattered salt on black rock. He pressed into her again, his heart on her lips.

Is that what it is, he wondered, thinking of love? *Could this be it?*

EIGHTEEN

The softball game was set for six thirty, to end at dusk. Corey came via bus, and the short walk over to the softball fields west of the water tower, looking lean and sinewy in long shorts and a loose sleeveless shirt.

Jude sniffed. "Is that aftershave you're wearing, Corey Man, or did you soak in a bath of rose petals?"

Corey shook his head as if forlorn, made no reply. "You sure they'll let me play?" he asked.

"It's just a game," Jude answered. "Really, who's gonna stop you?"

Slowly the players gathered, some coming directly from work, others pulling up in cars, lugging coolers. It was a warm, still night. Jude introduced Corey to his coworkers, guys like Ivan, DaJon, and Billy. Corey and Roberto greeted each other like long-lost Ping-Pong partners.

Roberto turned to Jude, grabbed him by the shoulders, and solemnly intoned, "As my hero Ron Burgundy said in *Anchor-*

man, 'For just one night, let's not be co-workers. Let's be co-people.'"

Corey's gaze turned to two girls as they approached the field. "Is this her?"

Yes, it was. Becka Bliss arrived with Daphne. They had become friendly of late. Becka wore gym shorts and a three-quarter-sleeve baseball jersey, with a Mets hat screwed backward onto her head. She looked like an athlete, ready to play, and cute as a puppy. Daphne's hair was pulled back, showing the fine, porcelain features of her face. Her shirt was under-size, revealing a toned, tanned belly. It was one of those moments that occurs when a seemingly ordinary girl—someone not on the male radar, which scans the seas like a nuclear sub, *ping, ping, ping*—shows up one day and blows everybody's mind. A revelation that most often happens in September, after a nine-week summer, and ends with an astonished question or two: "Did you see Daphne? How'd that happen?"

The game was hardly an athletic contest. Just various people joking around, making ridiculous plays, standing in the outfield with beers in hand, more worried about spilling than catching, everybody laughing and having fun. Corey played exceptionally well, though, hitting long balls into the beyond, racing around the bases like a jaguar. Daphne seemed interested in him, and Corey enjoyed her attention.

"You like her?" Jude later asked Corey.

"Becka? Yeah, she's great. I love a girl who can turn a double play," Corey said.

"I mean Daphne."

Corey pondered the question. "She available?"

"Looks like you've got a shot. You think you can get a ride home?" Jude asked. "If Becka and I . . ." He didn't finish the sentence.

"Worst-case scenario, Roberto's got wheels," Corey answered. "I'll be fine, Jude. You two can go make out under the boardwalk, or whatever it is you wild and crazy kids do these days. Who knows? Maybe I can find a better-looking driver." He got up and wandered over to where Daphne sat, eased down beside her like Miss Muffet's spider, and the way she turned to him with an authentic smile told Jude he didn't have to worry much about Corey's ride home.

After the game, folks dispersed in different directions. Corey and a large group, including Daphne, headed over to the boardwalk at Field Four. Jude and Becka veered away from the crowd, at the stage in their new relationship when they sought only each other, and walked barefoot to the Atlantic's rim. Becka had brought a big blanket and wrapped it cozily around their shoulders, huddling close. As they moved away from the lights of the boardwalk, Becka gazed up at the night sky. "So many stars," she said, "and a quarter moon. It's beautiful, Jude."

They stopped at the crest of the dry sand, before it sloped down to the surf, and laid out the blanket. Becka said, "They say each star is a soul looking down on us."

Jude gazed up, wondering. "So if you die?"

"You become a star," Becka told him. "My mother says that people don't *have* souls; we *are* souls."

"So you believe in God?" he asked.

She looked at him in full seriousness. "I believe in magic."

A new mood settled over Jude, a restless, wordless quiet, and he thought of Lily, his lost sister. He considered the stars above.

I wish I may, I wish I might . . .

"What is it?" Becka asked. "Sometimes you get this look on your face, and it's as if you're far away."

Jude had only told Corey his secret. His family knew the truth, of course. But now, for reasons he could not fathom, he felt the locked-away words begin to form somewhere in his belly, rising up to his mouth, some inner demon to exorcise. He wanted Becka to know.

Listen:

Jude lay with his back on the blanketed beach and said, "Can I tell you something?"

He felt his body beside hers, his bare arm against her soft skin. They were alone together—together, and yet still alone—the sand beneath them, cooling in the night air. It felt good to be with her in this way. He sighed, ready to begin. "You know about my sister, Lily . . . Little Lil, we called her."

Becka squeezed his hand and her good heart cracked, the way ice on a winter pond spiderwebs when you step on it, when you can almost feel yourself plunge into the frozen water. Yes, Jude's sister, Lily. A depth of sadness she never knew.

Nothing ever in her world had touched that kind of sorrow. The loss of a sister. It felt foreign, exotic—a feeling she had never felt. Yet it excited her, this physical nearness to something so sad and important as the death of a child. So she waited for the words to shower down like blue rain, his voice like a doomed poem dropping from the sky.

"It was my fault," Jude said. And he said it without emotion, flat as the horizon, four ordinary words like soldiers in a line. *It was my fault.* He glanced sideways at her to see if she understood, then looked up and away, as if confessing to the summer sky above. "She died because of me."

"Jude."

"No, it's true—let me talk, okay? I want to tell you. In my family, you see, there was always this idea that if we didn't say the words, if we didn't say it out loud, maybe it wasn't real. Just, you know, nobody move, nobody talk, and nobody gets hurt. We were, like, all sitting in a blackout—no lights, no candles, total darkness, and we pretended it was somehow okay. Lil was dead. And we just went on living in that darkness, bumping into each other, apologizing constantly, falling down, getting hurt, saying 'sorry' and 'excuse me' and 'don't worry, it's fine.' Saying 'please, forgive me,' and 'accidents happen.'"

His voice sounded urgent and bitter now, not like him at all. Jude was opening a cellar door for her, inviting her down the creaky stairs into some dark place of his soul. It frightened Becka. She released his hand, her entire body tense and listening.

Jude continued, "That's all we kept saying: 'It was an accident, no one's fault—these things happen for a reason.' God, I hated that one. *Happen for a reason.* What total bullshit."

"I don't understand," Becka said. "You said—you told me yourself—she drowned."

"That part's true," Jude said. "I was there. I was supposed to be watching her—but my mom was gone for so long, and it was so hot that day, must have been ninety-five degrees. Lily loved the water—we had a pool in our backyard. She spent hours splashing around in her orange floaties."

Becka listened now to his breathing, the way the words came out in spurts and declarations. He was still next to her, here at the beach, and at the same time impossibly distant, a chasm she could not cross. Above, the stars were pinpricks of pale yellow lights on a velvet cloth, and she longed to be that light shining down for him.

"That was my job: 'Watch Little Lil till I get back,' my mom said. And she went off in the car. I didn't know where. I still to this day don't know for sure where exactly she went; I can only guess what was so important. All I know was she left me alone with Lily, and it was my job to take care of my sister."

"How old were you?"

"Nine," Jude said. "Lily had just turned four."

"Nine years old? She left you alone, watching your sister by yourself?"

"I did it plenty of times," Jude said defensively, his voice jagged now, ragged and uneven. Worn out already.

Becka half turned, propped on her left elbow. She brushed the hair from his face, saw the sharp sickle of moon reflected in his eyes.

He shook his head, shivered a signal: *Don't.*

Becka looked at his eyes—they were fixed on some distant elsewhere of the imagination, as if watching something that existed only in memory.

"I was in a recliner by one end of the pool," he said. "It was hot, and I was bored and tired. I had this handheld video game, and I was determined to reach the next level. Lily was paddling around in this rubber duck inner tube, you know, those rings that go around your waist?"

"Yes, I know," Becka said, her voice a hush, a shush. She wanted to kiss him now, cover his mouth to keep the words from pouring forth. And at the same time, she knew what he needed from her, and so she listened.

"It was so weird, because I didn't even notice at first. I never heard a sound. I never saw her slip through. . . ." His voice snagged on the memory, caught like an animal in a snare.

She heard him swallow, breathe deep, determined to continue. "And I can picture it so clearly." He lifted up his hand like a sleepwalker moving down a darkened hallway, and let it drop to his side. Empty.

She reached for his hand and squeezed. "You don't have to—."

"I want to," he answered.

And though Becka wished he wouldn't go on, wouldn't speak

more of it, she asked him, "Please, it's all right, you can tell me," because she knew he must, just as it was her necessity to bear witness to this confession. He was the mouth, the soft lips to her ears, whispering the horrible truths.

"I saw that duck floating in the pool, Beck—it was blue and yellow—and it didn't register at first. I watched it float past, an inflatable duck in the water, and it took me a moment before I realized Lily had slipped through. I just watched it like a dream as it drifted past, merrily along."

Becka waited, spoke nothing.

He finally said, "Then it hit me. *Lily.* I stood up, searched the water, and I saw her on the bottom of the pool."

There it was, he'd said it. Rockets didn't explode, the world's roof didn't cave in upon him. There were still stars twinkling in the night, little souls in yellow dresses, and Becka still by his side.

A flickering light reflected off his wet cheek. She dabbed it with her thumb, brought it to her lips. "When you cry," she said, "I taste salt."

NINETEEN

Corey and Jude just goofing around. They hadn't seen a lot of each other the past week. Jude had been busy with work and with Becka, while Corey—somewhat spectacularly—had gone on a couple of quasi dates with Daphne. The days just flew; July arrived full blast, furnace blowing: Life was good, better than ever.

Tonight Corey was over at Jude's house, hanging in the basement, gaming, eating junk, shooting the breeze.

"Where's the party at again?" Corey asked.

"Gilgo Beach," Jude answered for the third time.

"And whose house is it?"

"Are you my mother?" Jude cracked.

"Just answer the question, Jude."

"Ivan Kozlov—he works at West End Two with me. You met him at the softball game," Jude explained.

"Kind of a nervous guy with high-maintenance facial hair? I think he plucks his eyebrows."

"That's him," Jude replied. "Ivan's parents are divorced, father supposedly has this amazing house on the water, way out on Ocean Parkway into Suffolk County. Anyway, his father is away for the weekend, and Ivan decided to commandeer the house for the night. Says he's invited everyone he knows."

"Berto going?"

"Yeah, he's meeting us there."

"Sounds good," Corey said. He picked through some magazines on the table, settling on a *TV Guide.*

Jude checked the time. Daphne and Becka were picking them up in Daphne's car. It turned out that Daphne was a catch in more ways than one. She didn't drink, smoke, or curse, so far as Jude could tell. That is, she was the perfect designated driver for a Saturday night. For all her waifish, bee-stung-lipped beauty, Daphne turned out to be a total brainiac, with ambition to become a veterinarian. Who knew?

"Did you know they showed movies on the Weather Channel?" Corey asked, incredulous.

"No, I did not know that," Jude replied. He was distracted by a video game, versing some kid in Taiwan.

"Well, I guess they do," Corey said, shaking his head. "There's a whole article about it. That's, like, so lame."

Jude had just died on a planet with two moons. Shot through the heart. "What movies are they showing?" he asked.

"I don't know—let me see." Corey riffled through the TV

listings. "Okay, okay, fine. *The Perfect Storm*—I get that. *March of the Penguins*? What's the *March of the Penguins*?"

"That's a pretty good movie, actually," Jude said. "It's about—"

"Don't tell me; let me guess," Corey interrupted. "Penguins, marching, right?"

"Corey Man, you're good."

Corey continued to scan the paper. "But, I mean, obviously, there's not that many weather-centered movies out there. Once you show, I don't know, um—what's another weather movie?"

"There's that one where they chase the tornados—with all the flying cows everywhere."

"Right, right, um, *Twister*!" Corey remembered, laughing. "And there was that other movie, when there's, like, a huge flood and New York City freezes over? They get trapped in the library and have to burn books to keep warm?"

"*The Day After Tomorrow*," Jude said.

Corey laughed. "We could totally do their programming for them. We'd put on *Cloudy with a Chance of Meatballs* on Saturday mornings for the kids. *Ice Age* would work, all the sequels. But after a while, I mean, look at this, on Friday night they are showing *Misery*."

"The Stephen King flick? I liked that movie."

"Yeah, but Jude, we're talking the Weather Channel. That whole movie is indoors, practically."

Jude gave up on the video game, dead again. This time his head got crushed by an alien with a moon rock. Corey was too much of a distraction. He tossed the headset onto the floor. "It starts with a snowstorm, remember? That's when he gets into the car accident."

"Yeah, but that's kind of a stretch, don't you think?" Corey countered. "What are they going to put on next? *The Godfather*—because it rains in the movie?"

"When you think about it—and for the record, I wish I wasn't—there's weather in every movie," Jude said.

Somebody flicked the lights off and on from the top of the stairs. Jude's father called down, "Jude, there's a couple of attractive young women here to see you. I told them they probably had the wrong house."

Oh, God, parents. Could they be any worse?

Becka and Daphne waited just inside the front door, looking around the room with curiosity. In that setting, the friends awkwardly said "Hey" all around and in every combination— Jude to Becka, Daphne to Jude, Corey to Daphne, endlessly— until Jude pushed open the front door and led them outside.

"Hey, before you go," Jude's father called after them, "where are you headed tonight?"

"A party," Jude answered. "Some kid from work."

"Not too late, I hope," his father said. "You know the rules, Jude. Be safe. Looks like rain tonight, slippery roads."

They walked to the car, the four of them together, Daphne

jangling keys, Becka half bouncing with eagerness. Jude glanced sideways at Corey and claimed, "Shotgun."

Corey gave his friend a stunned, hurt look. "Really?"

Jude laughed. "Just busting. Becka and I'll take the back. You can ride shotgun tonight, Corey Man."

TWENTY

Two cars on a narrow road.

Music plays from inside, mixed with young voices, laughter.

An animal crosses from shadows into light . . . a car drifts into the approaching lane . . . Daphne jerks the steering wheel . . . bones shatter . . . Becka staggers out from the backseat, battered head in bloodied hands . . . in the back, Jude groans, bleeding . . . and Corey, on the front passenger side . . . he's already gone.

Uncrash the car.

Push pause.

Hit refresh.

Delete the forever ever after.

PART TWO: AFTER

TWENTY-ONE

Jude, adrift. The days a monotonous drizzle, gray as slate. Food without taste, sun without heat. The days' events tumbled like laundry in a drying machine, a jumble of impressions and memory, mingled with bleached-out reality like faded photographs: the flickering glare of the television screen, the scrape of cutlery across awkward dinners, clumsiness of spilt drinks and hurried apology, dark hallways and closed doors, clouds and sleet and whispered urgencies, the guttering flames of church-lit candles.

Corey was gone.

Could it be? Could such a thing have happened? Hadn't they just been joking around together, hitting golf balls into the void, playing video games, watching dumb movies, and laughing, laughing?

Jude felt drained, tired all the time. And yet he couldn't rest at night, took naps in the day. Falling asleep in a chair, head in his hands at the dinner table. Listless. None of the pieces of his life fit together; it was all scraps and fragments, shards of shattered mirror reflecting up from the ground in grotesque disorder. *Who am I?* Jude wondered. *And why?* He thought of Corey and of Lily. On some mornings, too many mornings, Jude found himself hunched in the shower, his eyes leaking tears, leaking life. He felt hollowed out, carved up like a jack-o'-lantern.

Jude remembered:

They had taken him away in an ambulance. But first, Corey. They rushed Corey's body the hell out of there, and Jude, banged up and broken, head fogged and clanging, sat and watched the vehicle *whirrr* away, red lights spinning. It hurt to breathe, and he wondered if it was worth the effort. Three splintered ribs will do that to a guy. And life too will fill a body with air and heartache. Too much, too much to think about. So he filtered it out, processed what he could, blanked out the rest.

When he was a kid, Jude had had his back molars pulled. The dentist's assistant placed a mask over his face. She turned a knob, smiled, and called it "sweet air," nitrous oxide, and soon they could yank and pull, and Jude didn't care. *Do as you please, good doctor. Yank away! Just keep that gas pumping.* He awoke in bed with the sweet taste of blood on his tongue, cotton stuffed deep into his swollen mouth. They gave him something for the pain. Yes, he remembered, the fog lifting. Clarity sweeping it away. "Something to knock the edge off," that's how they put it. He slept a dreamless sleep of unremembering. And when he awoke, more pain.

TWENTY-TWO

The funeral struck Jude as surreal, a bizarre theater production directed by a madman. He felt like a stage prop in a cardboard crowd of mourners. Cue the grieving friend wrapped in black. Maybe it was because of all the familiar faces, students and teachers from school, all doing their best to act appropriately, actors playing out a pantomime of grief. The girls in tears, the boys standing droopily around, faces blotched with worry, dressed in ill-fitting jackets and borrowed neckties. Trying so hard to act grown-up. Their pretty young faces made horrible by grief. Jude looked away. He didn't want to join his friends from school, talk to them, say all those hollow words that floated around the high-ceilinged church.

"*He was such a great guy.*"

"*A terrible tragedy.*"

"*It was meant to be.*"

Pop, pop, pop. The platitudes burst. The absolute fact of Corey's death destroyed them all. There was nothing to say, nothing for Jude to believe. And most surprising of all, Jude felt little at all, as if his nerve endings had gone dead. Muffled, deflated. There was a wound in his heart, and his soul seeped out, like air from a balloon. He stayed near his parents, filed down the aisle together, sat walled in between them on the hard wooden pew, knelt and stood when signaled. Mostly, he waited for the whole sorry performance to conclude.

It all seemed unreal. Despite the casket, the mourners, the fractured memory of that night on the road, Jude kept half expecting Corey to burst into the room, grinning and pointing, saying, "How good am I? How good am I?!"

Ha-ha, Corey Man. You really fooled us this time.

Minutes passed that felt like hours. And Corey didn't show. More time, more waiting. Still no Corey.

So this was it.

Corey's extended family filled the front three rows. Jude watched from behind, stared at the men's knobby necks, the women in hats, veils. Corey's parents stood tall in dignified grief, proud and full of grace, backs erect, heads held high: "Oh deliver us, Lord, from every evil."

Jude saw Becka across the pew and back, and other friends—Berto, Lee, Stallion—and was grateful when they hung back, did not move to console him. He couldn't deal with those guys, not now, not Becka. . . .

He watched it all with the eyes of a wounded bird that had fallen from its nest—Jude of darting eyes and busted wing. In this place, sanctified and sterilized, Jude's unspooling thoughts did not linger on Corey but instead circled back to that other memory, Lily's funeral, and the vision of her small body at the bottom of the pool. He remembered a blue-and-yellow rubber duck floating on the water, the mockery of its beaky grin. Jude gripped the pew's backrest and watched as his knuckles turned white. The old priest with large drooping ears like a basset hound's talked and tried to sooth the visitants, sought to explain, and asked, "If God is for us, who is against us?" God was not cruel, but loving. God was not indifferent, but compassionate, our savior and our strength. *Not mine*, Jude decided. He found no solace in the words, but instead felt resentment toward this empty ceremony. So up he rose and down he knelt.

"Let us pray," the priest said.

"Lord, hear our prayers."

Jude soundlessly mouthed the words and responses. And in the end, he felt like a carved piece of oak, wooden as Pinocchio, dreaming of becoming a real boy. Swallowed by the whale, in the belly of the beast, lighting matches in the dark. His mind felt vague, his thoughts unsorted. Tears came when the music filled the great room, and Jude did not move to brush them away.

He tasted salt.

Salt water.

And he wondered if Becka could taste them too.

Jude remembered swimming with her in the ocean. The trick was to get past the breakers. The waves would roll in one after the other like charging cavalry, curl and crash in clouds of white foam, and if you got caught unawares, a wave could knock you off your feet, and you were rag-dolling in a rush of surf. But if you got past the breakers, swam under and through, then the ocean became peaceful, undulant as rolling hills. Jude and Becka did that together—they made it through, together—floated on their backs, faces to the sun, and felt the rise and fall of the ocean's tidal hum. Jude remembered a line from a poem he had studied in school: "*Water, water every-where, nor any drop to drink*." In Jude's mind he reached out his hands and felt for Becka's fingertips, up and down they floated in the bath of salt water. Strange to think of it as a sea of tears closing around them, heaving them up, easing them under. Ebb and flow. Inhale, exhale. He opened his eyes and she floated away.

The ocean will make you sick, drive you crazy. You can't drink that water.

A hand fell on Jude's shoulder; his father offered a handker-chief. Tight-lipped, Jude shrugged it away. A weight pressed against his chest, his cracked ribs. The cage that protected his inner organs—kidney, liver, heart—had failed him. The music stirred something in his plum heart, some desolate place the words could not reach, and the bird had flown. He thought how one day he might write a song and use that same organ sound, figured on the spot how to transcribe the notes to guitar. The heart too was an organ. A pumping mass of muscle. It would be a song without words, emotion in each note's fuzz and intonation, the struck chord glimmering like a sun-blazoned ocean, like explosions in the sky, and he'd call the tune "My Sweet Zombie Boy."

At last it ended. They shuffled out from the pews, moved in small steps, feet barely lifted off the floor, toward the back and the reprieve of wide, open doors.

He saw Lee, square-shouldered and stupified. Vinnie stood beside him, a blurry mess. They looked at each other, like department-store mannequins across the aisle, in mute helplessness. Vinnie's lips quivered, his Adam's apple bobbed, eyes as lifeless as brown buttons.

"Jude," a voice said. Becka reached out a hand. She looked into his eyes, searched for something there. Jude pulled away, gave his head a quick shake—*not now.* He continued walking. There was still the burial to get past, the *interment*, as they called it. A hole to dig. More walls to build, dirt thrown over everything.

"I want to go home," he told his father. "The pills. My ribs. I'm so tired."

"But Jude," his mother started. "We still have the cemetery. Corey's parents."

Maybe there was something in his eyes after all, or perhaps it was the way he said it. His father intervened, "He's been through enough, Joan." And to his son: "Okay, Jude. Let's take you home."

TWENTY-THREE

"So where we going?" Jude asked.

Becka, behind the wheel, made a right on Merrick Road. "Nowhere really, just a place I like."

They hadn't seen each other since the funeral, Jude not even bothering to answer most of her text messages. If Becka was pissed about the blow off—and Jude guessed she was—she worked hard not to show it. Becka talked constantly, chittering like a squirrel about this, that, and the other thing. Nervous, keeping things light, avoiding the big topic. Jude looked out the side window at gas stations, delis, littered sidewalks, and faded pizza joints. She talked about things that happened at work, asked Jude when he thought he'd come back.

"I'm not," he said.

Becka frowned, braked at a red light. "Not at all? Not for the rest of the summer?"

"I might paint the house," Jude said. "My dad's been talking about it."

"You know how to do that?"

"Not a clue."

She stopped in the right lane, put on the turn signal and navigated a clean parallel park on the street. "Nicely done, don't you think?" she asked brightly.

"Mill Pond," Jude observed.

"Have you been here?" she asked.

"Sure."

"There's a loop trail we can take." Becka reached into the backseat, hoisted up a wicker basket. "I brought some yummy food."

Jude climbed out of the car. He didn't know the difference between a pond and a lake and figured that the guy who named this one didn't know, either. It looked like a small lake to him. Or maybe a big pond. Whatever. He seemed to remember that it had something to do with depth, not the size of the water but how deep it went. There were benches scattered around, a couple of rundown, splintery gazebos, and an aggressive gaggle of geese honking for food.

Becka led the way around to the right and into the woods. Jude followed a half step behind. Becka grew silent, pensive. And Jude waited for it to come.

"So how are you doing?" she asked. "I've missed you."

Jude shrugged. "About what you'd expect, I guess." He didn't give her much, didn't have much to give.

They walked for a while, about halfway around the lake, then found a small clearing across a wooden footbridge, a patch of grass where one pond flowed into the other. Becka set down the basket. The afternoon light on the fade, not a soul around.

They ate quietly, Becka uncertain, offering him food and apologizing for every little thing.

"It's good," he said. "I'm just not hungry."

Finally, it came. The talk about the accident and Corey and how sorry she was, how messed up everything felt between them.

"Maybe it was meant to be," Becka offered.

"No, don't say that," Jude said. "Don't say that."

Becka looked away. She saw a feral rabbit across the field moving cautiously in the late-afternoon light. *This is the time they come out*, she thought. *Safer in the dusk.* She wondered why that was. Fewer hawks this time of night? Or just less people out, clomping around, talking in loud voices, laughing stupidly, walking dogs?

Jude rose, paced around the fringes of their conversation. This was Becka's show, this little get-together in the park. She wouldn't let him be when that was all he had wanted, to be left alone. "You know I hate it when people say that," Jude continued, waving a hand dismissively. "*Meant to be.* What's that even mean, anyway? You really think this was some kind of master plan, Becka, a car wrapped around a tree?"

Becka stayed silent, regretting her mistake. He had changed before her eyes, now all jittery and jangled. She had said too much already.

"People die," Jude said, agitated. "Terrible things happen every day. Accidents. Good, kind, beautiful people die all the time. Babies in cribs. Kids with cancer. Mothers in supermarkets drop dead in the frozen food section, clutching boxes of fish sticks. And the best anyone can do is hand me that bullshit line, 'meant to be.'"

"It's not a line," Becka protested. She spoke in a soft, conciliatory voice. "I was in that car too, Jude. So was Daphne, remember? We're all trying to understand it just like you. Please," she said, gesturing to the blanket, "sit down."

Jude latched on to the word. "'Remember'? *Remember?* Like you think it slipped my mind?"

"Jude, I didn't—"

"And as for Daphne," Jude interrupted. "Do you really, really think I care? She killed my best friend."

"It was an accident, Jude. Don't you dare blame her," Becka said. "She really liked Corey. You saw them together. How do you think Daphne feels?"

Jude paused, momentarily caught off guard. He grinned with malice. "An accident? Or was it meant to be? Huh, Beck? Which is it? Because you can't have it both ways," Jude bullied. He waved a hand dismissively. "These easy explanations. Does it make you feel good, Beck? Does it help you sleep at night?"

"Jude, please."

"'Jude, please,'" he mocked.

Hurt flooded her eyes. Becka busied her hands, packed

away the failed picnic. Wrapped tinfoil around the chicken. Sealed the grapes in Tupperware; they went bad so easily.

"You believe in God, is that it?" he asked, probing for a weakness, talons out. "How nice."

Becka cast her eyes downward, sat in stillness, waited for the shadow to pass. She looked into the cruel mask of his face. There was no light in his eyes. The kindness drained out. "I do," she said scarcely above a whisper. "I believe in . . . something. I don't know, Jude. It can't all be for nothing."

"But that's the whole point!" Jude exclaimed. "Nothing makes sense. We could all be wiped out tomorrow, and the sun would still come up. Because nothing matters."

"I want to leave now," Becka announced. She rose to fold the blanket.

Jude did not offer to help. "I can't do this anymore," he said. "We should take a break. Picnics in the park. Jesus Christ."

Becka felt punctured, stabbed in the chest. "You don't mean that. Do you, Jude? Tell me you don't mean it."

Jude dared not look in her eyes. He clenched his fists, full of fury.

"Tell me you don't mean it," she repeated. Becka tried a different tact. "You're upset, Jude. You've been through so much."

"I'm not 'upset,'" Jude replied, more mockery in his voice. "*Upset*? You're kidding me, right? You think I'm upset? What am I? Some kid who dropped his ice-cream cone, is that what you think?"

"We have to stick together, now more than ever. I can't do this alone."

"It's done," he said. "I'm sorry, but . . ." He turned his back to her. "I can't do this, Beck. I just can't."

She let him leave, watched him go across the grass back toward the path that led to the car. Jude needed time. He'd be all right. They'd be fine. He just needed time, that was all. An inner voice advised: *Stay strong, hang back. Don't let him see you cry.*

The gray rabbit lifted its head, paused, and watched the approach of the figure's dark threat, then darted beneath a bush.

Safe.

TWENTY-FOUR

The next morning, Becka left a note in Jude's mailbox. His mother found it, set it on the kitchen counter. A sealed white envelope with JUDE written across it.

"Girl can't take a hint," Jude grumbled to himself. She kept trying to drag him back. He carried the envelope up to his room, flopped on his bed, and tore it open.

> Jude,
> I remember when I was three or four years old, my parents took us camping. It was a good time. I played with my brothers in a rocky stream, climbing on the slippery rocks. We ate s'mores by the fire at night. Matt hit a Wiffle ball into the thick underbrush, and because I was the smallest, they made me crawl in to get it. That's when I found my plastic cowboy, half covered in dirt. I thought it was the greatest

discovery ever, and I loved it. Stupid, I know, but I still have it up in my room. Just a plastic cowboy. But to me, finding it was like a miracle. A gift. Now why am I telling you this, now that it seems like we've come to the end? Because that's how I feel about you.

Love,
B

Jude felt his chest pound. He knew that it must have been a difficult thing for her to write. He wondered about that last part, "Love, B." They hadn't said that word before, and he wasn't sure what it meant exactly. But just the same, he felt it too, knew it was the right word.

Just the wrong time.

TWENTY-FIVE

On Jude's desk in his room sat a new laptop computer. It was a gift. For school, senior year, then college. All those big things ahead he didn't care about anymore. The laptop was beautifully designed, fully loaded, the best Mac on the market. There was a time, not long ago but a world away, when such an unexpected gift would have brought a smile to his face. He'd feel grateful, maybe even offer up some big show of affection for such a hug-worthy present, create a Hallmark moment with the folks—Mom and Dad and Jude in a warm embrace. *Love, love, love all around.* They had somehow seen into his secret heart and, unannounced, provided its desired thing: a damn laptop. And so Jude was supposed to look at his parents and ask with glee, "How did you know? How did you know what I always wanted?"

Hey, they were trying. He realized that. But he couldn't, or wouldn't. No, that's not right, not exactly. Jude was trying too, clawing for air, but it wasn't working, no uplift in ordinary things, his lungs waterlogged, sinking under a sunken feeling.

Jude sat on his bed, staring at the computer where it had sat, untouched, for the past three days. His father had unpacked it while Jude sat there, watching. He was still their little boy, and this was his parents' attempt to throw him a life preserver. They were firm believers in stiffening the old upper lip, burying the past, and moving on.

And Jude thought, *This is what you get two weeks after your friend dies. Bad things happen to you? Don't worry, gifts to follow.*

Karma with a two-week lag time.

He rose to his feet, walked to the laptop, lifted it up, carried it back across the room. Jude slid open the bedroom window with his one free hand, gave the computer a toss into the afternoon air, just to see if it could fly. Poor thing, no wings. Maybe someday they'll make an app for that.

Motherboard smashed, keyboard crunched, LCD screen shattered. He thought of other things he'd thrown away, and people too. It felt good to be free.

Jude didn't care if he ever saw Becka again.

His father soon came storming up the stairs and burst into the room apoplectic, arms waving. "What the hell, Jude?" he shouted. Jude's mother pushed in behind her husband, so that now the three of them stood staring at each other, agape. Jude couldn't remember the last time they'd all been in his room at once. It made his space feel small, cluttered, a place he'd outgrown, like the hallway of an old elementary school.

"You're paying for that!" Mr. Fox demanded, pointing out the window. His voice cracked with emotion. And just as quickly, he seemed to sag, a huge exhale, the juice drained out of him. He sat on the corner of Jude's bed, head down. "I know it's been hard," he said to the floor in a soft voice. He looked up, blinked, searched Jude's face for some sign. Jude looked away, guarded. "You can't shut down on us, Jude. I won't allow it." Mr. Fox turned to his wife, as if startled to see her standing there. He reached for her hand. "We won't allow it."

Jude imagined that his father's words were little silver fish swimming about the room. *Glub, glub, glub.* He closed his eyes and saw one swim into his ear and out the other. He felt its silver fins shiver against his consciousness. And so came three thoughts in close succession.

There was a crash.

His parents heard it.

And now it was time to get those two the hell out of his room.

TWENTY-SIX

Jude squandered most of the next week on the couch, remote in hand, blitzing through the channels. Sometimes he didn't pause on a single station, just cruised through flashes of light and color, and he'd roll through them all two or three times before resigning himself to some game show or *America's Funniest Videos.* The idea was not to think or feel, just go dull and dim like a mushroom in the rain. There was a long list of things not to think about.

He sensed, however, a change in his parents; they hovered more, seemed newly solicitous, circling him like moths around a porch light. One early evening, Jude lay on the couch, a blanket pulled up to his chin, mangled bag of chips on the coffee table. His father sat in the leather recliner, leafing through a magazine. But out in the kitchen, his mother banged ominously, rattling dishes, slamming drawers, simmering.

She marched into the television room, just stood there like an announcement nailed to the wall, angry at the television, raging at fate, staring at Jude, then back to the television again. "Jude, I haven't heard you play your guitar in the longest while." There was honey in her voice, but poison in her eyes.

Jude didn't stir. Returned his gaze to the television screen, as if something fascinating was happening there, instead of a commercial for some bank.

"Why not turn that thing off," she suggested. "Bring out the acoustic, Jude, play some oldies for your mom, Neil Young or something. You know how much I love the Beatles. Remember 'Blackbird'?"

Jude again made the slow, lazy effort of looking at her, swiveling his head. "I don't feel like playing right now."

"Get up and get your guitar," she snapped with surprising ferocity. "We've spent hundreds and thousands of dollars on lessons for you, and I'm not going to sit here and watch you throw it all away. Snap out of it!"

His father put down the magazine. "Honey," he cautioned.

"No, no, no," she said. "This boy has got to snap out of it. Jude, get off that couch and play guitar—now."

"Mom, what's wrong with you? I said I don't feel like it. I'll pay you back if it's about the money." Jude threw off the blanket and stood, making to flee.

"He walks!" his mother mocked.

"Why don't you go back to bed, Mom," Jude exploded. "It's better when you're zonked out."

"What did you say to me?"

"Joan, Jude, don't," Mr. Fox was on his feet now, palms open, beseeching.

She moved swiftly and snatched at Jude, her thin fingers clenched like a bird's claw on his upper arm.

He turned and glared at her, body coiled, hostile, vibrating.

"You can't talk to me like that—I'm your mother. You can't say those things!" she hissed, fingernails squeezing into his skin.

Jude yanked his arm away. He looked at his mother's red-splotched face, saw the sad crazy panic in her eyes, and he knew he had hurt her badly and simultaneously knew there was nothing he could do to make the pain go away.

Jude leaned in to her, and through gritted teeth said, "You don't know. You don't *understand* how I feel."

She staggered back as if pushed. "Jude," she whispered, "Don't you realize? I do . . . I know so well."

No, not Lily, Jude thought. *I'm not going there. This isn't about her.* He grabbed his iPod off a counter, stalked to the front door, pushed it open hard with a bang.

"Jude!" his father called. "Come back here—I want you to come back right now. Jude!"

And he ran. Barefoot. Ran without hope, without destination . . . ran to burn off the anger, ran as if he were chased. He started out too fast, puffing hard like a sprinter, churning through the changeless sprawl, the suburban streets named after Civil War generals, Sherman and Grant, Thomas and Meade. Then came the streets with the names of colleges, Princeton and Adelphi, Yale and Amherst. Finally his gait evened out, the strides became long and powerful, his breathing regulated. Becalmed. He stopped for a moment, flicked a thumb across his iPod, found Arcade Fire, and turned it up loud. *You don't know how it feels*, he thought. *How it feels to be me.*

TWENTY-SEVEN

Late that night, Mrs. Fox pushed open the door to Lily's room, the way fingers might gently probe a flesh wound, and found Jude, arms splayed, asleep on his sister's bed.

The boy did not stir, and so the mother stepped closer until she saw the heave of his chest, heard the air escape past his parted lips.

Standing there, watching her son sleep, Mrs. Fox seemed to break a little, another one of the heart's small fractures. She left, vanished into the hall like a whisper, and shut the door behind her. She returned to her own bed to stare at the wall with sand-dry eyes, no tears left to cry, her heart in ruin, thinking, thinking.

When Jude woke, he felt oddly serene. He'd never before slept in Lily's room, didn't even remember deciding upon it. He opened his eyes, saw Lily's things: framed photos, a poster of a cat on a limb with the words HANG IN THERE! printed in purple letters, drawings, picture books—*Goodnight Moon, The*

Very Hungry Caterpillar—a shelf of dolls, and stuffed animals. He stretched, touched the sacred treasures, allowed his fingertips to rest on Lily's photograph, landing softly on her smiling lips. He pulled open a dresser drawer. Girl colors, lavenders, pinks, and yellows. The clothes were neatly pressed and folded by the loving hand of his mother. Jude lifted out a large, brown folder from the bottom drawer. Bound by an elastic band, it was filled with Lily's artwork, drawings of cats mostly, with round eyes, pink triangle noses, and three straight whiskers on each side. He sat on the bed, leafing through the pictures one by one. Toward the bottom, Jude found a drawing that took his breath away. Two crude figures standing hand in hand, a yellow sun in the top right corner, a zigzag line of blue grass across the bottom.

Crayoned across the sky: I LOVE JUDE.

TWENTY-EIGHT

He found breakfast waiting for him on the kitchen table. A green place mat, white bowl, spoon, grapefruit, and folded napkin. A slender glass of orange juice had already been poured, and a box of cereal set out. Jude stood, looking at this, perplexed, when his mother entered the room. She was dressed in baggy clothes, old jeans, sleeves rolled up to her elbows, hair tied back under a scarf. "I hope cereal's okay," she said, not quite looking at him.

She turned and left the room, dragging a vacuum cleaner by the hose as if it were a reluctant dog on a leash.

Jude scratched his head, yawned, sat down. He poured himself a bowl of cereal.

His mother returned. "Here's today's paper. Those Mets, they'll break your heart."

Jude looked up at her in amazement, but again she was gone, off hunting for the furniture polish. They did not speak of last night's argument. No one apologized, no one sought comfort. It was a new morning. But Jude knew his mother, and knew that she had made a peace offering. He did the only thing he knew how: He ate the breakfast, drank the juice, and piled his dishes neatly into the sink.

Corey had been dead for twenty-seven days, and everyone—Roberto, Lee, Vinnie, even Jude's parents—agreed that it would be a good idea for Jude to get out of the house, try to have some fun. It was like a huge CIA conspiracy between them, but instead of overthrowing the government, their big goal was to get Jude showered and dressed. Baby steps, baby steps.

"Sounds like a plan," Jude finally relented. His voice flat, obedient.

So Jude followed his feet, hands at his sides, and went. It was Vinnie's fault mostly. He was the one who kept after Jude. He talked Jude into going to some big party in Guffy's woods, where there would be a log to lean on, a small fire, and a loose tribe of teenagers dedicated to the proposition of getting toasted.

The reason for this night's debauch—as if a reason were needed beyond the ecstatic double whammy of it's summer and it's Saturday—was some girl's seventeenth birthday. Susan something. And so a wide assortment of people Jude knew, and some he didn't know, were there to ring in the festivities. He arrived by car with Lee and Vinnie, the tragic trio reunited—to celebrate (or lubricate) they downed a six-pack before meeting up with the others—and traveled by foot down a wooded path. As they moved deeper into the underbrush and pines, Jude saw broken glass, tree limbs shot up by air rifles and BB guns, thick ruts made by muddy four-wheelers and hardened in the dirt, remains of old fires, crushed beer cans strewn along the way like so many dead soldiers.

The gathering was monstrous, more than fifty strong, way bigger than Jude had expected, and the sight overwhelmed him at first. Everybody was there. Even under normal circumstances, Jude wasn't a dive-right-in kind of guy. He gestured to a large fallen tree limb on the periphery. "Go ahead," he told Vinnie and Lee. "You guys scout ahead. Find out where the beer's at. Come back with refreshments."

"You okay?" Vinnie asked.

"Totally," Jude reassured him.

The party was well under way. Jude leaned against the log and watched the partiers laugh and flirt and howl at the moon. Well, that was mostly Terry O'Duffigan—the Duffmeister—who was already well-oiled. One guy climbed a tree, doing the Tarzan thing, trying to impress somebody, anybody, but old Jane was probably already off in the bushes with bigfoot. No one else seemed to care.

Vinnie came back fifteen minutes later, listing a little to the left, and plopped down beside Jude. *Could he be bombed already?* Jude wondered. Vinnie handed Jude a red cup filled with beer. He slipped an arm around Jude's shoulders. "I've missed you, bud," Vinnie said, a hint of a slur in his voice. "Where've you been? You never come out anymore."

"I know, I suck," Jude apologized.

Vinnie surprised Jude by hugging him, squeezing hard. He pulled back, stared at Jude a little bug-eyed, and whispered intensely, "I think about him every day." Vinnie kept on staring at Jude, waiting for something. "I'm really feeling messed up," Vinnie confessed, "ever since, you know," and his eyes rolled back in his head a little.

Jude realized Vinnie was already skunked. "Did you take something?" he asked.

"What do you mean?"

"Did you swallow a pill or something?"

Vinnie's head lolled a bit, and his eyes focused somewhere six inches to the right of Jude's forehead. "Less just say I'm feeling no pain tonight," he confessed.

"Careful," Jude said, but Vinnie didn't catch the words.

"You—you," Vinnie said, suddenly stabbing at Jude's chest. "He was your best friend. In the world. You guys were like—"

"I know," Jude said. They drank to Corey's memory and to friendship and to going to college in another year and getting the hell out of town.

"Partying is such sweet sorrow," Vinnie said, polishing off the last of his beer. He got up to work the crowd.

"Hey, Stallion," Jude called after him, "try not to fall into the fire."

"Oh, dude," Vinnie said, "I almost forgot. Freakin' Becka's here."

"Shit. She see you?"

"A little bit, yeah."

"She saw you a little bit?" Jude repeated. He couldn't keep from smiling. "What's that mean, Stallion?"

"It means I need another beer, my brother," Vinnie said, standing to full height. He adjusted his belt, burped, and part swaggered, part staggered back into the breach. One arm outstretched, empty cup leading the way.

Jude too needed another beer.

Becka must have gotten invited to the party somehow, obviously, a friend of a friend Jude guessed, and what did it matter, anyway? They weren't a couple anymore. Still, Jude felt a pang when he first spied her across the clearing, talking with a group of girls. She stood cross-armed, pulling on the skin of her elbows. Listened to someone tell a story, laughed a little. Her presence made Jude uneasy.

He found the keg, jostled with some guys, and there she suddenly was, at his side. "Hey, stranger," Becka said.

"Hey, yeah, Becka," Jude greeted. He filled her cup from the hose. "I didn't realize you knew . . . um . . . Susan something."

"It sounds like you're the one who doesn't know her," Becka replied. There was an edge to her voice, a hint of warning, as if she had sprinkled a handful of tacks on the ground before her feet.

Jude nodded, scanned the crowd. "First time I've been out in a while," he said.

Becka nodded, shifted her feet. She glanced back at her friends. "Look, I—," she paused, jerking a thumb toward her friends. "You take care, okay?"

"Yeah, yeah. I'll be around, party's just getting started," Jude replied. He leaned in for a moment, almost imperceptibly, as if for a hug or to kiss her on the cheek. Becka turned and twirled away.

"I'll be around too," she called over her shoulder. It didn't sound to Jude at all like an invitation.

Well, that sucked.

Later on, maybe a little drunk now, or maybe kind of a lot, Jude got to talking and laughing with Dani Remson. She looked crazy-beautiful, as usual, her skin smooth and radiant. Dani had dated Corey, briefly, and Jude saw the way she looked at him, the sweet empathy in her eyes, *poor Jude*, and he knew he could have her if he wished.

Dani must have noticed Jude glance in the direction of Becka. "I'm confused," she said. "You keep looking at her. Are you two, like, still a couple?"

"Were," Jude said. "It's over."

Dani smiled, flashing her perfect teeth. "Good."

Jude looked around, leaned into Dani. "This party—"

"—is played out," Dani said. She placed her hand on Jude's chest. "Maybe . . . a change of scenery?"

And without another glance back at Becka, or Stallion, or anyone else, Jude left the party with Dani Remson at his side.

That's the way things go sometimes. You want to hurt somebody—maybe a friend, maybe a stranger, maybe yourself—and, hell, you go and you do it. Some friends you bury, others you leave at parties holding a red plastic cup.

The next afternoon Becka stopped by the house without a word of warning. She arrived on the pretense of returning a few music books he'd lent her. Jude didn't invite her inside; she would have refused anyway, he could see that on her face. They talked out in the front yard, under the scraggly limbs of his butt-ugly tree. The scene felt about right, depressing as hell. Becka didn't appear that angry. *Over it*, he guessed. At long last, Becka straightened her shoulders, sighed a weary sort of resignation, and resolved, "I lost you out on that road, didn't I?"

Jude didn't argue. It had to be this way to make his isolation complete. He was traveling now between two steel rails running parallel into the distance. No steering wheel, no brakes. Jude followed the path carved out for him, gobbling up track, *toot-toot*. Get out of the way and nobody gets hurt.

Becka was the one who walked away after that, not looking back.

Deleted.

And nobody gets hurt.

Jude went inside, up the stairs, and climbed out onto the roof. It had become his alone place, a refuge he had formerly shared with Corey. Up there, above it all, he felt closer to Corey, remembered his friend more keenly. Up there, he wrestled with a world gone wrong. The pale sun dropped down to nest momentarily in a stand of high trees to the west before setting entirely. Sundown, sundown.

A car pulled up, idled in front of the house. Jude recognized it instantly. The dark blue, practical Ford. Corey's parents' car. The passenger door opened, a woman got out.

It was Jude's mother.

She leaned down, poked her head through the passenger window. Corey's mother was behind the wheel. In all these years, Jude had rarely seen the two women together. Here and there, maybe, but it's not like they were friends. *Why now?* Then Jude understood. It was obvious. Mrs. Masterson had buried a child. She was now a member of the club. Two mothers, brought together in shared recognition of their unspeakable grief.

The earth's ceiling turned crimson and orange, before deepening to blue and black, the sky a great bruise. Time passed. No stars yet, but Jude knew they were up there, needing the darkness to shine. That's what Becka told him: *each star, a soul.*

Jude lay on his back and waited for the darkness to

swallow him, for the stars to appear, for mourning to come. He couldn't pray, didn't have the words, didn't have the God, but he could grieve, and maybe that was a prayer of its own. Jude wondered, like Becka, why he didn't float off the earth and fly away. What anchor kept him tethered to this place?

TWENTY-NINE

Roberto at Jude's front door waving an envelope. "S'up, Jude," he said. "I thought I'd deliver your last check from work. You never came to pick it up."

"Oh, hey, thanks," Jude managed. "You didn't have to; they could have mailed it."

"Could've, would've," Roberto said. "I figured I'd bring it over, see how you're doing."

Jude waited for Roberto to hand over the check. It didn't happen.

"So how's it going?" Roberto asked.

Jude shrugged his answer.

"You going to invite me inside?"

Jude looked past Roberto's shoulder to the car parked by the curb. "Mom's Taurus, huh? I see you're still riding in style."

"Yeah, well, the red Lamborghini is in the shop," Roberto explained. "And I only drive the yellow one on Tuesdays."

Jude grinned, shifted his feet, opened his shoulders. "Come

on in," he offered. Jude led Roberto downstairs into the finished basement, which was set up with video games, a flat-screen television, Jude's music gear, places to sit.

Roberto whistled, head swiveling, taking in the room. "Wow, it's like a recording studio. You know what else you need down here?"

Before Roberto could fill in the blank, Jude reflexively quipped, "More cowbell?" The words slipped from his mouth out of habit. An old joke he shared with Corey. It was the first funny thing he'd said in weeks. But Roberto stared blankly. He didn't get the joke.

"What?"

"More cowbell," Jude repeated. "It's from the *SNL* skit. Will Ferrell, Christopher Walken, 'Don't Fear the Reaper.' Don't tell me you've never seen it." He looked hopefully at Roberto, who shook his head.

"I've got no idea what you're talking about," Roberto confessed.

Jude did his best impression of Christopher Walken, barking out lines from the skit: "Guess what? I've got a *fever.* And the only *prescription* . . . is more cowbell!"

Jude turned on the computer, a virus-infested IBM clone—he definitely regretted the Great Laptop Toss; what an idiot—and found the skit on YouTube. "I can't believe you don't know this," he said, shaking his head. Jude felt a jigger of old enthusiasm rising up inside him, an approximation of his normal self. For the next hour, the two boys swapped favorite funny videos pulled from the Web, cracking up over the dumb things people do.

Roberto's howling, cackling laughter was infectious. He talked up a stream of stories about life at West End Two. Adventures with Kenny, dumb lifeguards, surprise inspections, softball games, and postwork parties in the dunes. Roberto had a way of finding the comical in most things. "So get this," he said. "I walked into the back office and caught Kath sucking face with Denzel. I didn't know whether to pretend I didn't see it, go all invisible or something, or get in line. They should lock those doors is all I'm saying!"

Jude roared at Berto's bug-eyed delivery.

"This one's crazy, Jude, check it," Roberto said, leaning forward, gesturing with his hands in excitement. "Billy Motchsweller got arrested at work last week for selling ecstasy."

"What!"

"It was a whole freaking scene. So, like, he was stuffing the pills between the hamburger buns—that was his distribution system, see—and Billy accidentally sold to an off-duty cop!"

"Oh, my God," Jude said, stunned.

"He's so screwed, man," Roberto said.

"Well, I guess that explains the long lines," Jude commented.

"Never thought of that." Roberto chuckled. "Sales have really dropped off since the arrest." He pointed to Jude's gear in the corner. "That your guitar?"

"Obviously, you're not a golfer," Jude deadpanned.

Roberto laughed. He pulled a DVD off the shelf. "I can't believe you own *Plan 9 from Outer Space.* I love that movie!"

"Worst film ever made," Jude said. "Actually, I sort of inherited that copy from Corey. He brought it over one night and . . ."

A leaden silence filled the room, threatening to sink the lightness of the past hour.

"We should watch it," Roberto piped up. "Get some people together. Come on, Jude. It's a good idea. Corey would approve."

Jude shook his head, placed the movie back on the shelf. "I don't think so, not now."

"Another time," Roberto said. He glanced toward the stairs, pondering his options. "You were pretty trashed the other night at the log," he said.

"Yeah, I just—"

"—cut out with that girl," Roberto said, completing Jude's sentence.

The memory embarrassed Jude. He wasn't proud of it.

"You shouldn't have done that, Jude, with Becka there. That was cold."

Jude didn't try to explain, couldn't explain even if he wanted to. It was like kicking a dog. What could you say? The dog deserved it? He finally asked, "How is she?"

"Becka's good." Roberto paused, thinking it over. "Don't ask me, Jude. You've got her number."

"You think I should call her?"

"What do I know? I'm just a fat virgin," Roberto replied. "But, yeah, I think you should call. Absolutely."

"I screwed up," Jude admitted.

"Yeah, you did," Roberto agreed. "But there's been a lot of that going on. You've been dealing with stuff. I hate to see you guys end this way. Besides, now you're even, right?"

Jude remembered that night at the bowling alley. How he felt when he saw Becka with the drummer. A fatigue came over him; he could almost feel his face drain of color. "Look, I'm fried." Jude yawned.

Roberto took the hint. "Sure, sure. I was just leaving." They climbed the stairs together. Roberto paused at the front door, looked at Jude as if he had something important to say. "You're going to be all right, Jude."

Jude nodded, remorseful. "I know, I know. I want to feel better. . . . It's just . . . not easy, you know."

Roberto nodded, trying to know.

"What about Daphne?" Jude asked. He was surprised to hear the words come from his mouth. He didn't think he cared about her.

"Daphne?" Roberto smiled, his eyes a little more alive. He considered the question for a long while, looked down, tilted his head from shoulder to shoulder. "She's like you. Stopped coming to work. Went into stealth mode, you know. I've hung out with her a little lately."

Jude raised an eyebrow.

"Just friends," Roberto said, "my specialty." He paused, thought of something to add. "Daphne's applying to veterinary schools. All of them out of state. I think she wants to get as far away as possible."

The news made Jude feel glad. He felt a tremor in his heart. As if a deadened nerve ending twitched to life. It was something. A murmur. Jude stepped forward, held open the door. "Thanks," he said. "For the check, for stopping by. I mean it. You didn't have to come."

Roberto smiled. "It was Becka's idea. She still cares about you, bro."

Jude took in the news, accepted it as fact. Becka Bliss Mc-Crystal. She still cared, even after he'd given her every reason to give up on him. "Tell her . . . hey, you."

"'Hey, you,'" Roberto echoed. "That it?"

"That's it," Jude replied.

THIRTY

Jude had been painting the house for three days now—and hadn't yet dipped a brush into the paint can. The first step, in his father's words, was all about "surface preparation." That is, scraping off the old paint that cracked and peeled along the white trim. It was mind-numbing work, done with a metal scraper, a coarse pad, and an iPod on shuffle. To cover his eyes and head from falling flakes, Jude wore sunglasses and a floppy rain hat he'd found at the bottom of a closet, along with a damp bandana wrapped around his neck to keep cool. Becka would have laughed at the sight of him. "Comical," she would have said. Nevertheless, Jude enjoyed the work. He took satisfaction in laying down the drop cloth to catch the falling paint chips, steadily inching the ladder along the side of the house. It was put-your-shoulder-to-the-wheel labor, no heavy thinking required. And so the job gave his mind room to roam free, like a knock-kneed pony in a great open pasture.

The bizarre thing about death—besides the absolute,

heartbreaking, unfathomable horror of it—was that everyday life kept on coming, like a slow-moving river burbling past. It seeped into every corner, into his bedroom, the living room, and out into the streets. The universe didn't cry or regret; it just rambled on. Nothing changed, yet everything felt different. Friends sent text messages. His father knocked on his bedroom door, inventing ways to lure Jude out of the house. The world tugged on Jude's sleeve. He found himself rinsing the dishes in the sink, hauling the garbage out to the street, scraping paint. *From can to can't*. Wherever he turned, life chased him down, dragged him back to the land of the living. And that was the whole deal, Jude mused, standing high on a ladder, arms moving back and forth across the eaves. You had to ride that river all the way to the sea. Jude didn't believe the stories that the priests told in church, the myths they taught in Sunday school. He wished he could, but he could never get past the problem of how all those different gods, from all those different religions, could possibly be right. Somebody had to be wrong. Instead of belief, Jude cradled doubt. He carried uncertainty on his back, a burden of not knowing. As he scraped away at the surface of his house, Jude made a truce with that unknowing.

He still thought of Corey all the time, but the shape of those thoughts had morphed. It wasn't Corey in death; it was the positive memories, images of the friendship that endured. Time had not healed him, but it had eroded the bitterness in his heart. For the first time, Jude felt sympathy for Daphne, the driver of the car. She was a nice enough girl who dreamed of becoming a veterinarian, fretted over sick cats, and now had to lug around guilt for the rest of her life. Daphne had agreed to be DD for the night; she wasn't drinking, wasn't jabbering on a phone. It was a freak accident: An animal stepped into the road, and she crashed into the only tree within a hundred yards. It could have happened to anyone, should never have happened at all. *Could have, should have*: The universe yawned its gaping maw. Jude couldn't hate Daphne any longer. The whole thing required too much energy.

Around noon, with the sun at its height, his father came around to eyeball Jude's progress. "Take a break," he said. "Come for a ride with me. I have to run a few errands."

"I'm rolling here," Jude replied. "You go."

His father waggled the keys. "Come," he said. It wasn't a request. That's the way people talked to Jude nowadays, like they all knew best. *Whatever.* Though Jude had his permit, he declined the offer to drive. He sat in the backseat, talking baseball with his dad. A safe, easy topic. Mr. Fox pulled into a plaza off Sunrise Highway. He handed Jude a fold of money and a short list of grocery items. "Do me a favor, Jude, pick these things up while I get the paint."

Jude frowned, accepted the assignment. He pushed a creaky shopping cart into the vast, cool supermarket, steered to the fruits and vegetables section. He checked the first items on the list: *grapefruit, apples, bananas*. Jude noticed an elderly couple nearby. A shuffling, bent-backed man wore Coke-bottle glasses and a green Jets sweatshirt that hung loose around his frail body. He squinted to read the prices, appeared confused by it all, shaking his head as if in great sorrow. A stout, white-haired woman stood beside him. She appeared alert, capable, and sturdy. A tough old bird. Gently she spoke to her husband and placed a bag of oranges into their cart. They rolled away together. This nothing encounter somehow drove a stake through Jude's heart.

"Jude? Is that you?"

A familiar voice called to him. Jude turned to see Corey's mother. Mrs. Masterson looked elegant, a tall, thin woman dressed in a gray business suit with matching skirt and jacket over a bright blue blouse. "Oh, Mrs. Masterson. Hi."

"Jude, I haven't seen you for ages." Her eyes scanned the vicinity. "Is your mother with you?"

Jude held a grapefruit in his hand. "No, I'm . . . my dad's at the paint store. I'm supposed to pick up some grapefruit and stuff."

She smiled, glanced at the fruit in Jude's hand. "Well, that one's not ripe, it's too yellow," she instructed. Mrs. Masterson picked through a few grapefruits, talking as she did so. "You have to look for ones that are more orange in color. Like these. But check for soft spots; you don't want the fruit that's been bruised."

Jude held out a plastic bag and allowed Corey's mother to select six good ones. He smiled. "Good thing I ran into you."

"You must be excited about school starting next week," she said, her smile an act of determination, a choice. "Senior year."

"Senior year," Jude echoed.

"Are you all set with college?" It was the question that every adult asked kids his age.

"Not yet," Jude said. "My grades are good. I'm thinking about Boston, or the city, maybe for music. Applications aren't due until January. We'll see where I get accepted."

"You did very well on your SATs. I remember Corey bragging on you, he was so proud," she said. Mrs. Masterson lifted her chin after those words, forced her body to stand erect. "There's time to decide yet, no hurries." She touched his arm, squeezed. "It's good to see you, Jude. If you ever want to come around the house, just to visit, you know you're always welcome. Corey's accident was hard on everyone, and I worry about his friends, especially you."

He felt a warm pressure build up behind his eyes, looked away. She was worried about him, this woman who had buried her son. "Thanks, maybe I will," he answered, even though he knew he'd never make that visit.

"Have you been going to church?" Mrs. Masterson was devoutly religious, never missed a Sunday. Corey and Jude had joked about it many times, since she always insisted on dragging Corey along.

Jude shook his head. "No, I—"

"It's helped me," she said.

"I'm glad," he said, and he was.

She looked gravely into his eyes. "Are you okay?"

Ninety-nine times out of a hundred, Jude faked that answer. Shrugged it off, gave a line, walked away. But this time, he stood there, breathless, his vision gone blurry, eyes moist. Something inside him seemed to break, like a dam giving way. "No," he admitted, "not really," his voice tripping over the emotion, the sound scarcely above a whisper.

Her warm, dark hands came to him then—hands that felt soft and infinitely kind—and wrapped around his own hands. "I know, Jude, I can see it in your eyes," she said. "If you leave your heart open, God will find you."

They stood together in the fresh-fruit section, surrounded by oranges and bananas, a white teenage boy and a bereft black woman, her hands holding his, tears in both their eyes.

When will we ever stop crying? he wondered.

"I'm helping my father paint the house," Jude finally said, shifting on his feet, trying to regain some sort of balance. "And we're taking down some bushes and that old tree out front."

"That will brighten up the place," she replied.

"Yeah, I guess the roots were kind of screwing up the foundation," he offered, somewhat lamely.

"It's good to let in the light," she said. Jude understood that she was speaking in mysteries, not of trees, of things deep and spiritual.

Jude's cell sounded, an electronic riff from a popular song.

He grinned awkwardly, embarrassed. "My dad," he explained. "He's probably wondering what's taking me so long."

Mrs. Masterson signaled that she understood. Before parting, she asked, "Is it all right, Jude, if I hug you? Right here in the middle of the supermarket?"

"I wish you would," he told her, his voice a bleat in the wilderness.

THIRTY-ONE

Jude couldn't sleep that night. By one thirty, he still lay on his back, mind throbbing with the conviction that everything in his world had gone wrong. He forced himself to retrace his blessings, the people and things he would never wish away. But it didn't work. Some secret part of him that he dared not confess longed only for annihilation.

The idea of death.

Sweet oblivion. Jude felt the undertow pulling him, the riptide washing him out. He stared at the ceiling. Water filled his ears; he was drowning again. Jude felt with astonishing certainty that he would die right there in bed if he did not act, did not rise this very second to resist the grip that pulled him deeper into the gloom. He sat up, flicked on a closet bulb, and quickly dressed, baggy shorts and a Radiohead tee. He slipped down the stairs, stepped out into the night, and sniffed autumn's sweet decay.

He walked aimlessly, or so he imagined, down a desolate

street, then another, crossing into an empty playground where swings dangled uselessly. He reclined on a seesaw, arms folded behind his head, invisible to any passing cars. Jude tried to clear his mind, casting away thoughts and images, hoping to stay as empty as the unwritten pages of some tender, forgotten book. He thought of zombies and ghosts, and he thought of the living. Somehow the thoughts hoisted him up, like strong hands yanking on his collar, and he knew there was only this present moment, cast adrift in the here and now. He breathed in, he breathed out. He decided to believe in life.

Jude punched out a message to Becka: *Can i c u?*

Would she hear it? Could she possibly be awake? He waited for an answer. None came. He sent a second message: *Now, pls.*

It was useless. She must be asleep, the cell off. But Jude was determined. He couldn't *not* see her. Jude's body wanted to run, needed to run, and so he ran along the front strips of grass between sidewalk and street, his body energized, heart beating steadily—all the way to Becka's house, two miles away.

Jude paused outside, gathered small stones from the road. There was a light on upstairs, leaking from the hallway. He tossed pebbles at Becka's bedroom window. The window shuddered up, a head poked out. "Who are you?"

It was Becka's brother; Jude recognized him from the band at the bowling alley. Even in the dark, he looked pissed.

"Sorry, I must've got the wrong room," Jude called up in a whisper.

"What?"

"Where's Becka's room?"

"Are you freaking kidding me?" the brother asked. "I should come down and kick your ass."

Jude must have appeared like a sad, pathetic figure out there on the lawn, because the brother—Matt, that was his name—finally pointed a finger at the next window. "That's hers, dickwad." He slammed the window shut.

More rocks, more anxious waiting. At last Becka pulled the curtains aside, peered out, recognized Jude's shadow, and signaled for him to wait. A pair of car headlights snaked down the street. Jude retreated behind a tree, an intruder in the night. Becka opened the front door. He stepped from the dark, whistled softly, and she came to him in bathrobe and slippers.

"Jude, what are you doing here?" she asked, slumber still in her voice.

"I couldn't sleep. I've been out walking."

"And now you're here at three in the morning," Becka stated.

"I'm sorry, it was stupid; I wasn't thinking."

She looked searchingly into his face. Her fingers touched his cheek. "You look like hell."

"I'm so, so sorry," he said.

Becka turned to look at the house. She chewed on the

corner of her lower lip, deciding. "Wait here," she instructed. Becka went back into the house and returned minutes later fully dressed, holding a plastic bag and a set of car keys. "Let's go."

"Where?"

"Shhh," she whispered, moving to the car. "I don't want my parents to hear us. You'll have to push me out of the driveway."

She climbed into the driver's seat and put the Toyota into neutral. Jude lowered his back to the front grill and pushed. The car rolled easily down the incline, banking into the street. "Hurry," she urged. "Get in."

Becka turned the key and away they rolled—down the road, around the corner, the two of them hushed in the thrill of their illicit escape, safely away.

She handed him a soda, purloined from the fridge. Jude twisted off the cap. "Where to?" he asked.

"Give me a hit of that first," she said, reaching for the bottle. Becka took a deep swallow, burped faintly, and giggled. "God, I so love burping." She laughed and took another sip.

At a stop sign, Becka found something acoustic on the radio, a guy with a guitar. The suburban side streets were ghostly, the town at rest. Jude sat back and watched Becka scan the road with alert, roving eyes. "You're a good driver," he said.

"Thanks," Becka nodded. "Not that I need your approval." She smacked him playfully on the chest. Jude caught her hand, felt it against his heart, and held it there. After a pause, she pulled her hand away and returned it to the wheel.

"I made you a sandwich," she said. "You like mustard, right?"

It was real ham, cut from the bone, on a kaiser roll. Jude ate ravenously. "I didn't realize I was this hungry."

She glanced at him, satisfied, and turned onto the parkway, the car picking up speed, hurtling toward Jones Beach.

THIRTY-TWO

Becka led the way through the dark, down the long West End beach toward the ocean. Jude smelled the briny air, tasted seaweed on his tongue before the ocean's hum had even reached his ears. His vision limited to shades of gray and black, Jude sensed something in the distance that couldn't be seen, something vast and mysterious called the Atlantic. There was another world across it, and even greater mysteries beyond. He reached out for Becka's hand. They walked barefoot and together to land's end.

They found a lifeguard stand and climbed to the high, wide seat. "Okay, I'm listening," she said with a new edge to her voice. "Talk to me, Jude. What's going on?"

Jude didn't know where to begin. His mind was like that restless ocean out there, thoughts churning.

"I've been thinking about my sister a lot," Jude said. "It's weird, you'd think after Corey—I don't know."

Becka glanced at him, watched the ocean, waited.

Jude sighed, frustrated. Not sure what he wanted to say or what had carried them to this moment in time, on the beach, under the stars. "I helped carry her casket," he said.

"Your sister's?"

"I guess my parents thought it was poetic or whatever, I don't know. I remember that I told them I wanted to do it, but it wasn't true. I just felt like I should."

"You were nine years old," Becka said, "and you carried a casket?"

"I didn't do it by myself," Jude said, "I had help—my father, some uncles, my parents' friends. All I really remember was how heavy it was," Jude continued, staring into the ocean. "I didn't expect that part. She was only, like, forty pounds, but the coffin weighed so much. All I could think about was the awful weight of that box. With each step, I knew I would carry her like that forever."

The surf pounded in broken waves. Becka squeezed Jude's knee, her face in shadow.

"The memories usually come in colors," Jude continued. "I'll see a certain shade of yellow, maybe, and I'll picture her in that pretty little sundress she used to wear; or green, and I'll remember her eyes, like yours almost, Beck, and how they shined when she laughed. I can feel her slipping away, like an echo dying in the distance."

He paused. "I'm the boy who let her drown."

"It wasn't your fault," Becka said. "You never should have been put in that position."

Jude nodded. "I know that. In my head, I get it. But—"

"You have to forgive that boy," Becka said.

Jude shook his head.

"You were just a kid," she insisted.

Headlights appeared along the beach, a four-wheel jeep rolling down the shore.

"Security patrol," Jude said. "We shouldn't be here."

"Quick, jump down," Becka said. They leaped to the sand. There were a couple of long, seafaring rowboats tied face-down to the stand. "Let's hide."

They squeezed between the two boats, huddled close together. Jude peered out from underneath, watching the lights bounce closer, closer, until turning away toward the parking lot.

They lingered in the black womb of the boat's overturned belly, waiting for the coast to clear, an electric closeness between them. Becka found his mouth, and they kissed, and time seemed to disappear.

"He'll find my car," Becka realized, standing to brush the sand off her arms and legs. "We should go."

Jude glanced to the east. The sky was softening, turning pinkish, foreshadowing sunrise. He clawed sand from his hair. "Are we going to be all right?"

Becka lifted her shoulders, let them drop. She didn't know, and so couldn't say.

"I'm sorry for everything," he said.

Becka nodded, looked at her feet. "You really hurt me, Jude."

He swallowed those words, each one like a stone in his stomach. "I want to try to make it right."

"Sometimes I feel like I fell in love with a stranger," Becka confessed. "I can't be hurt like that again, Jude—not by you, not by any boy. I deserve better."

Jude didn't answer. He knew that he couldn't undo the hurt, couldn't black out the stars above, was helpless to un-crash the car. He touched her slender waist, wrapped an arm around her back, squeezed.

Becka trembled slightly, hugged Jude in return. "We'll see what happens, okay? But you have to tell me one thing," she said. "Tell me it's over with that girl."

"It's over," Jude replied. "It never started."

"You embarrassed me."

"Nothing happened," Jude said.

"Nothing?"

Jude looked from Becka to the distance beyond. Then back to her again: "Nothing that meant anything."

Becka pulled the hair from her face. "I think I could love you, Jude. But I've got all kinds of warning bells going off in my head."

Jude understood. Some things take time. No one could wish the hurt away. They walked back to the car. There was a parking ticket on the windshield. They had lingered too long under the boat. Jude paused beside Becka, reading the ticket over her shoulder. "I'll pay it," he offered.

"Sold," she answered, stuffing the ticket into his shorts pocket.

"Listen, do you mind if I stay?" he asked.

"Stay? Here?"

Jude jerked his head toward the Atlantic. "I want to hang around, see the sunrise."

"I have to get back before my parents—"

"No, I know," Jude said. "But will you be okay, driving home alone?"

"You really want to stay here by yourself? Won't your folks freak? How will you get home?"

"I've got my cell," Jude said, patting his front pocket. "I'll call 'em. Seriously, they'll probably just assume I'm asleep."

Becka looked from Jude's face to the ocean beyond, light beginning to soften the horizon. "I wish I could stay with you."

"Another time, maybe," Jude said.

Becka bit her lip, nodded. "I'd like that, Jude." She pointed to the west. "Look! A shooting star."

They watched it burn across the sky.

"Can I borrow that blanket?" Jude asked. "And do you have any more food in there?"

Becka rummaged through the backseat and uncovered a half-eaten bag of Doritos. "Here's some orangey goodness for you. It's loaded with vitamin C."

"Really?"

"No, it's pure garbage," Becka laughed, "but very tasty."

Jude leaned in, kissed Becka on the forehead.

"Be good," she said, climbing into the car.

"I'll call you, okay?"

She rolled down the window, nodded once, waved.

He watched her drive away, his heart quivering with new hope. Jude pulled the blanket around his shoulders, turned back to the shore.

He drifted eastward along the surf until he found himself standing alone, no one in sight except for a few fishermen, just now arriving from the parking lot. He stood, reflective, re-membering how Lily used to splash in the water, and that wild banshee squeal of hers like an exalted, silly goose. Just a four-year-old girl. He could feel his cheeks lift to a smile.

Jude walked ankle-deep, then shin-deep, into the ocean. The water was surprisingly cold, biting. The waves had quieted, rolled in light and regular, more like an ambitious lake than a vengeful sea. Last night's storm had passed.

He didn't know what would happen with Becka. Maybe that's why he needed to be alone on the beach, to watch the sunrise, to be okay with himself, despite everything. Sometimes life seemed impossibly hard, full of car wrecks and souls that shined like stars in yellow dresses. So much heartbreak and undertow. Jude bent down, picked up a smooth white stone, measured its heft in his hand. And he reached back to cast that rock as far as he could.

Just to see the splash.

AUTHOR'S NOTE

The initial idea for this book—the car crash as a pivot point, the central fact in the lives of these teenage characters—came at a time when I was teaching my oldest son how to drive. An accident on the road is every parent's nightmare. Yet it happens everywhere, and too often ends in heartbreak.

Some quick stats according to the Centers for Disease Control and Prevention: Motor vehicle crashes are the leading cause of death for U.S. teens. Teen drivers, ages 16–19, are four times more likely to crash than older drivers.

We all know that drinking and driving don't mix; and texting, too. Studies show that the presence of teen passengers increases the risk, as does driving at night, when the rate of accidents becomes three times higher.

Be careful about those distractions. Stay under the speed limit, buckle up every time you get into a car. Be smart. Be safe.